MW01134427

LAST
RIDE

A NOVEL

G. MICHAEL HOPF

DEDICATION

TO THOSE WHO NEVER QUIT OR GIVE UP.

"It is not the critic who counts; not the man who points out how the strong man stumbles, or where the doer of deeds could have done them better. The credit belongs to the man who is actually in the arena, whose face is marred by dust and sweat and blood; who strives valiantly; who errs, who comes short again and again, because there is no effort without error and shortcoming; but who does actually strive to do the deeds; who knows great enthusiasms, the great devotions; who spends himself in a worthy cause; who at the best knows in the end the triumph of high achievement, and who at the worst, if he fails, at least fails while daring greatly, so that his place shall never be with those cold and timid souls who neither know victory nor defeat."

- Teddy Roosevelt

PROLOGUE

OUTSKIRTS OF MILES CITY, MONTANA TERRITORY

AUGUST 17, 1888

Blood was everywhere.

Every inch of Colton's cherished cabin was covered in thick sticky blood. It was splattered on the walls and pooled on the dusty wood floor. On the table, his wife lay dead, the blue dress he'd last seen her in was soaked with it, telling him she'd been attacked the day he left her.

He stood in shock, unable to move towards her, the grisly scene taking control of his motor functions and freezing him just inside the threshold. His eyes were locked in an unflinching stare with hers; he hoped to see movement, but none came. She was dead for sure.

Finally breaking free from his trance, he rushed to her side and began to sob. "Oh my dear, my dear Martha. Who would do this to you, who?" He cradled her lifeless body in his arms and wailed in grief. "My Martha, oh my beautiful wife."

Colton had left the day before to go into town and get provisions; but an unforeseen thunderstorm with heavy rains and high winds quickly moved in and forced him to overnight at the hotel. Sometime in the hours he was gone, someone had come and savagely murdered her. But who? Who would commit such a barbaric crime? He had an idea who might have done it, but would they stoop to murder?

Theirs was a special kind of love uncommon during that time. He was a white man and she a native of the Cheyenne tribe. They had met four years before when he had begun trading wares he'd imported from Seattle on the Cheyenne reservation. Not long after he asked for her hand, but her father refused. Out of respect he stopped pursuing her, but that didn't stop her. She ran away and joined him, knowing she'd never be able to return to her people. For him she gave up everyone she knew and everything she'd ever known, including her birth name, Asha. If she were to live with a white man, she'd adopt a white name and took Martha.

She had made him the happiest man, but he knew she had made quite the sacrifice. Thinking they could begin a life in town, he'd introduced her to his friends and associates. What happened next, he hadn't seen coming. The locals, friends and all, didn't approve; in fact, many expressed their displeasure. Over time his business was affected; the natives didn't want to buy from him nor did the locals. In less than a year he shut down his storefront, and together they found refuge from the ridicule just outside town on a three-acre plot with a small cabin. There she'd gotten pregnant and gave birth to a baby boy they named James.

The next year was a happy one. Marth and Colton felt complete with James, and on the business front, he had opened up trade with towns farther out. This took him away for extended periods of time, but Martha was more than capable of taking care of herself and James. During one of Colton's trips, two men from the Big Circle Ranch stopped at the cabin and harassed Martha; their unwelcome visit was cut short when she ran them off with a shotgun. Outside of that one incident, everything was going well until James came down with the flu; five days later he was dead. Following James' death, Martha fell into a deep depression. She'd given up her family and people to be with Colton and create their own family only to have that cut short.

Colton tried his best to console her, but it was a fruitless endeavor until one day upon returning from a business trip he found her like he'd met her, upbeat and happy. He wasn't sure what had happened during his absence, but he didn't much care; his Martha had returned.

Fast-forward six months and now she was dead—murdered. Was it those ranch hands? Could it have been her people coming to exact revenge? He wasn't sure, but he was determined to find out and bring the perpetrators to justice.

Familiar with how to prepare a body for burial, he slowly unfastened each button with care until he'd removed her dress; then he took off her undergarments, stopping when he saw the numerous wounds on her torso. Tears flowed when he imagined the terror and pain she must have experienced. Her upper body had suffered eight puncture wounds, which he could only assume were done with a knife or other sharp object. A seven-inch-long horizontal cut on her lower abdomen went deep enough to expose her intestines. *Was that the first wound or last?* he wondered. Her hands and arms showed physical trauma as well, no doubt due to her trying to block the attacker's knife blows. The final wound, the one that ensured her death, was the deep cut across her slender throat. He examined her privates, and it didn't appear she'd been raped; he found this a Godsend, the one positive development out of it all.

He took a deep bowl, filled it with water, grabbed a washcloth and soap, and bathed her body. When he was done, he put her in her favorite dress. With her body cleaned and dressed, he wrapped her tightly in a white sheet then carried her outside and laid her on the ground.

Digging the grave proved to be arduous due to the hard rocky dry soil commonly found in eastern Montana. After hours of work, the grave was an adequate depth and ready to receive her. He placed her shrouded body inside then proceeded to place wildflowers along with some of her most cherished personal effects next to her. When he was finished, he stood above the open grave and looked longingly down on her. Tears flowed freely and his hands trembled.

He opened a Bible and read a few verses; then he recited some prayers in her native tongue. With the ceremony over, he covered her body, hammered a cross at the head of the grave, and went back to the cabin to gather his things. He was headed back into town to first speak with the marshal; after that he'd begin to search for the one responsible for his beloved's death.

***

Colton walked into Marshal Franks' office and cried out, "Someone murdered my wife!"

Franks and one of his deputies, a man by the name of Seth Grimes, were playing cards on a desk. They looked up, but when they saw it was Colton, they went back to playing as if no one were there.

Colton raced up to the desk and barked, "My wife, Martha, she's been murdered."

Franks looked up and asked, "What makes you say that?"

Shocked by the question and the tone, Colton said, "'Cause she's been murdered, damn it. She was stabbed many times, her stomach cut open, and her throat slit."

"What would you like me to do?" Franks asked as he placed a card down, his focus on the card game not Colton.

"I want you to go find the men who did it," Colton said.

"Remind me again where you live," Franks said.

"Seven miles outside town, along Flatbush Creek," Colton answered.

"You said it right there, outside town. You see, Colton, that's out of my jurisdiction. I'm the town marshal. You need to go see the county sheriff; he'll take care of you."

"But the county sheriff isn't here; I heard he's in Helena until mid-September," Colton said.

"Then I suppose you'll have to wait." Franks

chuckled.

Seth let out a laugh.

"You think this is funny? My wife was murdered savagely by someone, and you won't lift a finger to help me?" Colton asked, shocked by the treatment he was receiving.

"A savage was killed savagely," Franks quipped.

"Damn you, Marshal!" Colton snapped.

"Whoa, watch your tongue, or I'll have you arrested," Franks barked.

"You're despicable, you truly are," Colton blared, his entire body shaking with anger. "When the sheriff does return, I'll tell him how you violated your oath of office. I'll tell him, you'll see." Colton turned and headed for the door.

"Stop!" Franks hollered.

Colton froze and stood.

"I'll help you. Come back here," Franks ordered, throwing his hand of cards down on the table. He got up and went to his desk.

Hopeful, Colton returned and stood at the head of Franks' desk.

Franks pulled a piece of paper and pencil from the top drawer. He looked up and asked, "What happened?"

"I returned to the cabin this morning and found my Martha spread out on the table. The blood…it was everywhere," Colton said, his voice cracking with emotion.

"It wasn't suicide?" Franks asked.

"No, it wasn't suicide. She had eight or more stab

wounds in her chest and her stomach…her guts were hanging out. No, it wasn't suicide."

"Any idea who might have killed her?" Franks asked.

"My Martha was so sweet, I don't know anyone that would want to do what they did to her…" Colton said and paused.

Noticing his pause, Franks asked, "What is it?"

"There were these two ranch hands; she embarrassed them a few months back. I suppose they could have come back and taken revenge on her."

"What two ranch hands? What happened?" Franks asked, genuinely curious.

"From the Big Circle Ranch, two ranch hands came by the cabin and gave her a hard time. My Martha was sweet, but she didn't take stuff from anyone. These men were up to no good, and she put an end to it. They made some veiled threats then left."

"When was that?"

"Seven, maybe eight months ago," Colton answered.

"Do you have any names?" Franks asked.

"She said one of them went by the name Jed, that's all I remember. That has to be a lead. How many Jed's can there be that work at the Big Circle Ranch?" Colton said.

"I know Jed," Seth said from across the room.

Colton turned and asked, "You do?"

"Yeah, but I don't see him causing trouble like you described. He never struck me as a man who desired after a squaw."

"Ignore him," Franks said, cracking a subtle smile at

Colton's expense.

"Are you going to help me, Marshal?" Colton asked.

"I'll run by the Big Circle Ranch and have a talk with Jed," Franks said, putting the pencil down.

"And?" Colton asked, hoping he'd get more information of timing.

"That's it for now. If I find or hear something, I'll let you know," Franks said. He got up and walked over to Seth's desk, where he was now playing solitaire.

"You come get me right away if you hear anything?" Colton said.

"Goodbye," Franks hollered.

Colton exited the office but didn't feel like he'd find justice for Martha. He just couldn't trust the marshal to do it right. He knew how he and the other townspeople felt about him and Martha. He knew finding her killers would be on the bottom of any list. What he needed was an incentive, a way to get everyone looking for those responsible for her death. Out of the corner of his eye, he spotted a wanted poster. He walked up to it and saw at the bottom a bounty was offered. His eyes widened as he knew what he needed to do.

CHAPTER ONE

ROCKLAND, IDAHO TERRITORY

AUGUST 21, 1888

Grant Toomey exited his single-level, ranch-style house and stretched. He looked out on the five acres of potato plants and grunted at the thought he'd have to begin harvesting. "George, get out here!" he hollered.

George, his fifteen-year-old son, raced out the front door, wiping his mouth as he went. "Yes, Pa?"

"It's time to get to work," Grant said.

"Great," George said with a tone of excitement.

With a bewildered look, Grant craned his head towards George and asked, "You really enjoy farmin', don't you?"

"Love it, Pa," George replied.

"That's your mother in ya." Grant snorted.

"I miss her," George said, his jovial tone shifting to melancholy.

Grant touched George's shoulder and said, "We all do, son. I think about her every day. She's with the Lord now, and we must keep on livin'." Grant wasn't lying, there wasn't an hour during each day since her death that he didn't think about Latanne, the beautiful French maiden who had appeared into his life at the right time and became the catalyst for the life he was living now.

George lowered his head but didn't reply.

"Margaret, come here," Grant called out.

Margaret was his thirteen-year-old daughter, and she was as spunky as they came. Hearing Grant call, she stepped out the front door and asked, "What is it, Pa?"

"Come and look," Grant said, motioning her over with his left arm.

She stepped over next to him.

He wrapped his long arm around her shoulders and drew her close. "I wanted you to see this beautiful day beginning."

"Looks like every other day," she quipped.

"It may appear that way, but each day is unique. Each day gives you a new lease on life, a new chance to turn it all around…"

"Are you about to tell us the story about how you met Mama?" she said in an anguished tone.

He chuckled and said, "You know me too well."

"I have much to do inside, got to do wash today," she said.

"One day you'll appreciate the lessons and morals I teach you. It's those lessons that you'll have when times get tough," he said before dropping his arm.

"I know, Pa, love you," she said, jumping up and kissing him on the cheek. She darted off just as fast, disappearing back inside the house.

Grant began to cough. It was so bad, he turned away from George, who was still standing next to him.

"You okay?" George asked, a look of concern on his face.

Finding a couple of seconds' reprieve between

coughs, he waved at George and said, "Go to the barn. Get started."

"Yes, Pa," George said and sprinted off.

Grant's coughing grew more intense. He pulled a handkerchief from his pocket and brought it to his mouth when he felt he was about to cough something up. He spit into the handkerchief and pulled it away to look. Splattered on the white linen was thick bright red blood. He looked around to make sure neither one of the kids was looking before folding it back up and shoving it into his pocket. This wasn't the first coughing fit he'd had, though this was the worst. He'd never had blood appear, and the sight of it scared him. Knowing he wouldn't be able to function today if his thoughts were plagued with his malady, he cleared his mind and set about starting his day.

ROSEBUD, MONTANA TERRITORY

"Remember everything I've taught you. After you've cocked the pistol, raise it to eye level and aim. While you're aiming, begin to apply pressure to the trigger with your index finger. Make sure you squeeze, don't pull," Billy said to Abigail, his seventeen-year-old niece.

Abigail held the Colt Single Action Army with both hands, her right index finger on the trigger and her left eye closed. Her target was a bottle positioned on a tree stump some ten yards away.

Standing just behind her, Billy softly whispered, "Maintain your sight alignment, sight picture and squeeze."

"Uncle Billy, ssh, I know how to shoot," she sweetly said with a slight admonishment in her voice.

"If you can't handle my slight distractions, you'll never be able to handle a gunfight," he countered.

She thought about that and went back to focusing. Today she was going to shoot not just one, but six bottles, one after the other, as fast as she could.

"You know what to do, now do it. See yourself hitting all those bottles," Billy said.

Always a good student and avid listener, Abigail followed Billy's instructions to a tee. She applied the correct pressure on the trigger until the pistol fired. The .45-caliber bullet exploded from the muzzle and struck the bottle, blowing it into thousands of small shards and pieces. She quickly cocked it, aimed, squeezed, and let loose another round; once more it hit. She repeated this four more times, striking each bottle. "I did it, I did it!" she cried out with joy.

"That you did. Now do it again," Billy said, pointing to the next group of bottles on an adjacent stump.

Abigail reloaded, readied herself, and took aim.

"Sight alignment and sight picture, then squeeze," Billy whispered behind her.

Instead of squeezing the trigger, she jerked it hard in anticipation of the shot and missed the bottle. "I missed!"

"Pay no mind, cock and keep shooting. Don't fret over your last shot, focus on your next," Billy ordered.

Abigail did as he said. She cocked it, took a deep breath, and aimed. She let her surroundings melt away until all she saw was the target and her front sight dancing a figure eight in front of it. With her finger on the trigger, she began to apply firm and even pressure.

"Focus, breathing, squeeze," Billy softly said.

The pistol fired. "That startled me," Abigail said, looking downrange at the shattered remains of the bottle.

"That's good it startled you. When people try to anticipate the gun firing or get impatient, they pull the trigger; doing that forces you to jerk, and the bullet usually won't hit the target like your first shot did," Billy explained.

"Can I keep shooting?" Abigail asked.

"How about we eat some lunch?" Billy asked, reaching for the pistol.

She handed it to him back strap first and said, "Thank you for teaching me to shoot."

Billy holstered the Colt and said with a broad smile, "Of course, everyone needs to learn how to shoot, even the fairer sex. In fact, women need to learn their way around weapons more than a man. There's a little saying that goes like this, 'God created men, Sam Colt made us equal.'"

"I like that," Abigail said, pulling some of her bangs down to cover her bruised and blackened eye.

"C'mon, your aunt Nell has some leftover biscuits," Billy said, draping his arm over Abigail's shoulders, and escorted her to his house.

Inside, Abigail washed her hands in the kitchen basin and took a seat at the table.

When Nell saw her niece, she cried out, "Girl, did

that man hurt you again?" She reached across the table and brushed her bangs away from her face.

Abigail recoiled and snapped, "Don't do that."

"Billy, you need to go talk to your brother. Hitting a young girl, especially your daughter, is unacceptable!" Nell barked at Billy.

"I've talked to him, but I'll do it again when I take her home," Billy said, taking a biscuit from a plate in front of him.

"Why did he hit you now?" Nell asked Abigail.

"I don't want to talk about it, please," Abigail said, her head hung low.

Nell got to her feet and walked around the table, stopping when she was behind Abigail. She bent over and embraced her. "I'm so sorry. If you were my beautiful daughter, I wouldn't treat you that way. Your father is a horrible, horrible man."

"He's just upset that mother died is all. He gets drunk and doesn't know what he's doing," Abigail said.

"Leave the girl alone," Billy said, chastising Nell.

Rubbing Abigail's arms, Nell replied, "It just makes me see red. That man is evil, and there's no excuse for it." She walked back to her seat and sat down. "I'd better not hear you didn't talk to him."

"Woman, enough, let the poor girl stop hearing all this chatter. I'll talk to my brother. Now can we say grace and eat?"

"Very well," Nell said, lowering her head to pray.

***

When lunch was over, Abigail went to help Nell. "Sweetheart, you're so nice."

"Thank you for taking care of me. I don't know what I'd do without you two," Abigail said, putting her head on Nell's shoulder.

"You've always got a place here, you understand?"

"I do," Abigail answered.

"Abby, come outside," Billy said, exiting the house.

"Go. I'll finish up here," Nell said, motioning for her to leave.

Outside, Billy was sitting in his favorite rocking chair, a pipe in his hand. "Take a seat."

Abigail sat next to him in a familiar rocker and nervously placed her hands on her trousers.

"Your clothes, that's what your father doesn't like," Billy said, commenting on the fact that Abigail preferred to wear trousers versus dresses.

"They're more comfortable is all. What does it matter?" she asked.

"There's what's proper and what's not," Billy answered, lighting his pipe and taking a few puffs.

"Wearing trousers doesn't make me less of a woman," she said confidently.

"Now, Abby, I agree with that. It's just that your father, he's sensitive to what others say…"

"It's more than that, Uncle Billy. He's just mean. I know what I said earlier, but he was mean even before Mama died," Abigail said.

Billy rocked in his chair, looked out towards the expansive fields of tall grasses, and sighed.

"I'm afraid to go home," she confessed.

"I'll talk to him, I promise," Billy said.

"Please don't. That'll just make him angrier," she replied.

Billy pursed his lips and thought about how he could handle his younger brother, Evan.

"Tell me about your days as a gunfighter and bounty hunter," Abigail said.

Billy cut her a glance. He could tell she didn't want to discuss her violent home life; she wanted to escape her world, and right now she could do so by listening to Billy's tales of adventure. "Have I ever told you about the meanest and most ornery bounty hunter that ever rode west of the Mississippi?"

"Never, please do," she begged.

"His name was Abraham 'the Hammer' Tillis, and your uncle Billy had the chance to ride with him for a while. You could say I was his protégé. I learned a lot from him...the good traits, you could say," Billy said, rocking back and exhaling a plume of sweet-smelling smoke.

"Good traits?" Abigail asked.

"Tillis was a real mean son of a bitch when he needed to be, and I say that as a compliment. He was an excellent bounty hunter, always got his man, but a few times he skirted the law but not enough to get him locked up. Last I saw him was sixteen or so years ago. He was headed to what is now Idaho Territory to farm; I think the town was Rockland. He met a nice French lady; she tempered his wild side, got him to stop drinking, cussin', and even got him to put away his irons. He's livin' there under an alias, name is Grant Toomey, on account of something that happened in Colorado back in '75. I suppose he doesn't want anyone to find him."

"Tell me a story about him," Abigail said.

"There was this time we were in Abilene—"

"Where's that?" she asked.

"Texas, near the panhandle," he replied. "We were lookin' for this vicious old bandit who went by the name Crooked Nose Cal. His claim to fame, besides his crooked nose, was he held up stagecoaches. He'd always kill the men, no matter what, and had the women sometimes do horrible things. When Tillis heard he'd mistreated the women, he was hell-bent on tracking him down. You see, when you're out there on the range there's a code, even with outlaws, that says you treat women respectfully; yeah, you can rob them, take their jewels and such, but you never touch them, no violating them."

"So there is honor among thieves," Abigail said.

"There is; you can rob someone without abusing the women and children. Anyway, where was I?"

"Tillis was hell-bent on getting Crooked Nose Cal," Abigail answered.

"Yep, that's it. He was, I swear he saw red. I remember when he told me we were gonna hunt him down, it didn't matter if they paid him, he'd make sure that cowardly bastard was taken down."

"So what happened?" Abigail asked, on the edge of her seat with anticipation.

"We tracked him down, took us about three weeks, but we cornered him at this old shack near this dry creek. We could've gone in and gotten him with no problem, but Tillis made us wait until Crooked Nose went to use the outhouse. You see, he wanted to kill him while he was on the pot, you know, humiliate the man."

"Did you get him?"

"Yep, we sure did. Tillis snuck up, threw open the door, and found old Crooked Nose with his trousers around his ankles. Tillis didn't try to arrest him. He put three bullets in him, two in the chest and one—"

"In the head, like you told me," Abigail said, proudly remembering some of Billy's lessons on gunfighting.

"Not today, it was two in the chest and one in the crotch. In fact, he shot there first." Billy chuckled as he swayed back and forth, a big smile on his face as he recalled that moment seventeen years before.

"Ouch," Abigail said, grimacing at the thought.

Overhearing a bit of their conversation, Nell shouted, "Darn it, Billy, are you telling that girl inappropriate stories again?"

"Ah, c'mon, Nell, the girl is practically eighteen," Billy complained.

"It's okay, Aunt Nell, I've heard worse," Abigail said.

Nell appeared suddenly. She stood above Abigail, wiping her hands on an apron. "Stop filling the poor girl's head with tales of your past. Running with outlaws and getting into gunfights is not something a girl should be listening to."

"I like it, Aunt Nell, I really do. I wish I could go be a bounty hunter and shoot bad men," Abigail replied.

Billy smiled when he heard that.

Nell shook her fist at Billy and said, "Look what you've done."

"Shall we go do some more shootin'?" Billy asked Abigail.

Abigail sprang to her feet and said, "Yes!"

Slowly rising due to his bad knees, Billy said, "Grab my holster. I'll meet you out there in a couple of minutes."

Not hesitating, Abigail hurried off to get his holster and gun belt. When she had it, she raced to the spot where they'd been shooting and waited.

Billy showed up a few minutes later, carrying a wood crate. He set it on the ground and pulled out another holster and gun belt. He handed it to her and said, "This is for you."

"It is?" she asked, taking it.

"It's yours," he said.

"Like, to use or to have?" she asked.

"To have, on account your eighteenth birthday is only a few days away," he said, bending down again. He stood back up, holding an unfamiliar Colt pistol. "Here, this is yours now too."

Her eyes widened with shock. "Uncle Billy, are you serious?"

"I am. I wanted to give this to one of my own kids, but as you know, we never had any. Being that you're like a daughter to me, I thought it fitting you have it," he said.

Abigail gently took the pistol and held it in both her hands as if it were a newborn baby. "It's beautiful. The barrel is short," she said, noticing the length was at least two inches shorter than the other Colt she was used to shooting.

"The man I got that off of must have had it cut down and new sights put on. I believe it's a five-and-a-half-inch barrel."

She held it up with one hand and aimed at the stump. "Boom," she said, mocking the sound of a gun firing.

"Let's shoot your new pistol," he said, handing her a box of bullets. While she was loading the gun, he walked down and set up a few bottles and returned.

With her new pistol loaded, she took aim and remembered everything he'd told her about the basic fundamentals; slowly she squeezed until the pistol fired. Like before, her aim was true. The bottle shattered. Not waiting for him to say anything, she quickly cocked it and shot again, once more striking a bottle; then again and again. She cycled through the entire cylinder, emptying the pistol.

"Hot damn, girl!" Billy shouted happily.

"Uncle Billy, I love this pistol," she said, her face beaming with joy.

He returned her smile and said, "I think you're ready to learn how to quick draw."

OUTSKIRTS OF MILES CITY, MONTANA
TERRITORY

Colton heard the sound of hooves outside his door. He flung it open to find Marshal Franks and his deputy Seth dismounting their horses.

"Marshal, what have you found out?" Colton asked, excited to receive a positive development concerning Martha's killer.

"Good afternoon," Franks said, walking up to Colton.

"Well?"

"Well, I spoke with Jed. He denies ever coming out to your property. I'll be honest, he seems like a nice young man. I agree with Seth that I don't see him as the man responsible for killing Martha."

"Are you sure?"

"What about her family? I know she left the reservation without her father's permission. Could they have something to do with it?" Franks asked.

"Never, her father would never have done that to her, never; whoever did this had pure hate in their veins," Colton said.

"Then we're at a dead end. I'll keep asking around, but without any evidence, I just don't know where else to look," Franks explained.

"Are you sure you spoke to the right Jed?" Colton asked.

"I'm sure, because there's only one, and he's Boyd's boy," Franks said. Boyd was the owner of the Big Circle

Ranch and a powerful figure in the area, some going as far as saying nothing could get done without his say.

"Maybe he's a good liar, and let it be known, I don't care whose son he is," Colton said.

"You should care. Boyd has much influence around these parts, you should know that," Franks scolded.

"Are you telling me that even if the Jed I speak of is the killer, there's nothing I can do about it because his father is Boyd Wallace?" Colton asked.

"No, I'm saying that you can't implicate anyone, especially a member of a prominent family, with no evidence. I spoke to him and that's that. He says he was in town with his friends, drinking," Franks countered.

Frustrated, Colton blurted out, "I'll find them. I'm paying seven thousand dollars to anyone who finds and brings Martha's killer to justice, dead or alive, even if it is Jed."

"You're putting out a bounty?" Seth asked from his perch in his saddle.

"Yes, I ordered the posters the last time I was in town. They should be sent out tomorrow morning," Colton said.

"Now hold on, don't you think that's premature?" Franks asked.

"I'm doing it, Marshal. I won't rest until my Martha's murder has been avenged," Colton snapped.

"You're seeking revenge. What happened to the justice you said you wanted?" Franks asked.

"Isn't it the same thing?" Colton asked.

DENVER, COLORADO

"Augustus Bryce Clemens, please come forward," said the superintendent of the orphanage, a priest who went by the name Father Harris.

August took a single step, stopping inches from the front of the desk. Standing at six feet two inches, he towered over Harris, who sat beneath him at the desk. He combed his slender fingers through his thick dirty blond hair then smoothed it out with his palm. A nervous energy ran through him. Today was the day, it had finally come.

Harris lifted his head from the file and peered over his spectacles. With a sneer, he said, "Today is your final day here at St. Ignatius Orphanage."

"It sure is," August said, a grin appearing on his clean-shaven face.

"It sure is...Father," Harris growled, reminding him to show respect for his position.

"How long is this going to take?" August asked.

Annoyed, Harris sat back in his chair and gave August a leery eye. "Master Clemens, the law requires me to let you go. If I could have found the courage and if my conscience allowed it, I would have let you leave these halls years ago. I'm not sure what came over you just after your fifteenth birthday, but it's almost as if the devil himself took possession of you."

"Are you going to bore me with more devil this, devil that talk?" August chuckled.

"You're insubordinate, and your attitude will not be

missed," Harris said, picking up a pen, dabbing it in an inkwell, and signing the top page in the folder. "There, you're now free to leave."

"Give it to me," August said, holding out his hand.

Harris scowled at the arrogance. He opened the right desk drawer, pulled out a small leather pouch, and placed it in August's hand.

The weight was heavy, telling August there was quite a bit of money left over from his parents' estate.

"You can leave now," Harris said.

"Thank you, and I hope I never see your ugly face again," August said. He turned and marched out of the office without a care in the world. He was happy to be gone; he had hated living there since he'd arrived eleven years ago. His parents had both been murdered, and with no other family, he was taken there and had spent the past eleven years angry at the world, angry at the men who killed his parents, and plotting this very day, because today he'd begin the journey to find those men. However, before he could do any of that, he'd need a horse, guns, ammunition and clothing. He exited the main entrance, which spilled onto a bustling sidewalk. The energy and vibrancy of Denver was instantly intoxicating; there was activity and people coming and going in all directions. There was so much to see and an endless parade of street vendors or shops to go visit.

The first person he saw, he asked, "Where can I buy pistols and a horse?"

The man gave him an odd stare and walked on without answering his question.

August approached the next man and asked the same question.

This time the stranger was helpful, gave him detailed directions, and went on his way.

August smiled broadly as he paused to take in the moment. He was finally free. Free to live life however he chose, and here he was setting out to fulfill a pledge he'd made to himself to track down the men who had murdered his family and deal justice in the only way that he thought was right...kill them.

CHAPTER TWO

ROSEBUD, MONTANA TERRITORY

AUGUST 22, 1888

"Abigail, open the damn door!" Evan, Abigail's father, hollered as he banged on her bedroom door repeatedly.

A stream of blood coursed down from Abigail's nose and dripped off her chin onto the dusty floor. Using the sleeve of her shirt, she wiped the blood from her face, grunting from how tender her lip and nose felt.

Evan had returned that morning from drinking all night, and instead of getting some sleep, he'd walked right up to Abigail, who was preparing breakfast, and began to slap her. As he beat her, he'd repeated the mantra he'd been spewing for seventeen years—that she'd killed his wife.

His words caused her more pain than any slap or punch. Being held responsible for killing your own mother was mentally anguishing for her. She'd never had the opportunity to meet her mother because she had died within minutes of giving birth to her. It was a fact that he never allowed her to ever forget.

"Leave me alone! I hate you!" she wailed.

"I swear, I'll kick this door down and beat you to within an inch of your life. Now open this damn door!"

"Leave me alone," Abigail wailed in fear, her knees pulled up tight to her chest as she rocked back and forth, her body pressed against the far wall.

Evan kept pounding on the door.

Abigail wiped the tears from her eyes. She looked at her window and thought about fleeing to Billy and Nell's house like she always did; then she spotted her new gun belt and pistol. Thoughts of pulling the Colt from the holster and using it against her father suddenly popped into her head. *Should I just kill him?* she asked herself. Her eyes darted back and forth between the window and the pistol. She knew if she ran away, she'd only end up back at the house and be at the receiving end of another beating, or she could pull the Colt and end the cycle of torment and abuse once and for all.

"I'm not giving you another chance. Open this door now!" Evan blared.

Abigail bolted from her spot and grabbed the gun belt. She took the Colt by the grip but hesitated from breaking leather. By killing her father, her life would forever change; yes, she'd be free of him, but would she be tried for murder and hanged?

"I'm gonna count to three!" Evan yelled as he pounded and jigged the door handle.

She tried to play out the various scenarios of killing him, but each time she imagined it would end with her swinging from a rope.

"One!" Evan hollered.

Unable to find the courage to kill Evan, she opened the window and began to crawl out.

"Two!"

She hesitated again as she thought about killing him

then running away. By the time they found his body, she could be halfway across the country.

"Three!" Evan shouted, stepping back and with all his might kicking in the door.

Wood snapped and broke as the door exploded inward.

Abigail saw her father standing there, his fists clenched and ready to be used as weapons against her. She leapt from the window and hit the ground running.

ROCKLAND, IDAHO TERRITORY

Grant woke to knocking on his door.

"Pa, you awake?" Margaret asked, and by the sound of her voice, she was concerned.

Grant rubbed the sleep from his eyes and instantly noticed the sun was riding high in the sky. He bolted straight up and called out to Margaret, "I'm up, I'm up."

"George is out harvesting, and I have breakfast on the table. It's covered up but cold," Margaret said.

"I'll be right there," Grant said, swinging his legs out of bed. When he got to his feet and stood, an uneasy feeling swept over him. Dizzy and unsteady, he promptly sat back down and shook his head in an attempt to rid himself of the vertigo.

"Pa, you okay?" Margaret asked from the far side of the closed door.

"I'm fine. Now go tend to your chores; I'll be out shortly," Grant said, hoping she'd leave him be.

Heeding him, Margaret went back to the kitchen.

"What the hell is wrong with you?" Grant mumbled under his breath. He could only imagine this feeling, coupled with the heavy, sometimes crushing fatigue he'd get lately, had something to do with his cough and bloody phlegm. Determined to get up and start his day, he struggled to his feet and slowly got himself dressed. The vertigo began to subside, and by the time he opened his bedroom door, he was almost normal, minus a burning in his chest. He made his way to the kitchen and found Margaret cleaning the dishes.

"You must have been real tired," Margaret said, her head down, focused on scrubbing the cast-iron skillet.

"Yes, I was," Grant said, unwrapping the plate on the table to find crisp bacon and two fried eggs. He picked up one of the eggs, now cold, and took a bite.

Margaret looked over her shoulder and said in a scolding tone, "Utensils, please. We're not animals."

"I'm trying to make less mess for you," he replied.

She rolled her eyes and said, "If you're going to eat with your hands, best take it outside."

"Yes, ma'am," Grant quipped. He placed the bacon and remaining egg in the napkin and folded it up. Before he exited the house, he walked over and gave her a peck on the cheek. "Thank you for taking care of your old man."

"Someone has to," she joked.

Grant chuckled and headed out.

Margaret finished the dishes and proceeded to her next daily task, which was tiding up the bedrooms. She had already taken care of George's room, so only Grant's remained. She pulled a curtain aside and let the mid-morning sun wash across the room. She grunted her disapproval as she picked up his dirty trousers and shirt off the floor. "He's like a child," she blurted out. She saw the tip of his handkerchief sticking out of the front pocket and pulled it out to find it covered in dried blood. Shocked, she questioned where that much blood had come from. She couldn't recall him complaining about a cut, but then again, Grant wasn't one to really complain. Brushing aside her concerns, she grumbled under her breath, "The blood will never come out."

DENVER, COLORADO

August opened his eyes to find the prostitute he'd slept with along with two large men standing above him. He shot up, half naked, from the bed and reached for the newly purchased 1875 Remington Army Outlaw revolver only to stop when he heard the cocking of a pistol near his head. "If you're going to rob me, just do it, but leave me the gun."

"We're not robbing you, we're kicking you out," the man holding the pistol said.

"Huh?" August asked.

"Your time is up; you've got to go. We need the room and the whore," the man grumbled.

"Oh, I see, yeah, sure. Let me get my clothes on," August said, sliding his legs out of bed and onto the cold hardwood floor. He looked up at the two men still hovering and asked, "Can I get dressed in private?"

"No," the man with the gun replied.

"I'll just be a minute," August countered.

The man looked at the other and nodded. He gave August one last glance and said, "Two minutes, tops."

"I hear ya," August said.

The men exited the room.

"I tried to wake you, sweetie, but you weren't moving," the prostitute said.

August winked and said, "That's okay. This capped off a great night."

"So where ya going?" she asked.

"Up to Montana Territory," August replied, slipping on his boots.

"What's up there, family?"

"You ask a lot of questions." August laughed.

"It's my job to know what my customers want, so I tend to ask a lot of questions."

"Makes sense."

"Why don't you stay an extra day or so and come back to see me," she said, rubbing his shoulders.

"Oh, I'd love to, but it's time for me to go. I have a rendezvous with a couple of men, and I don't aim to be late for my appointment."

"So you're a businessman of some sort, huh?"

"No, not that, but I do have some business to attend to with them," August said, standing and slipping on his shirt.

"What sort of business is that?" she asked, lying back on the bed with her legs wide open in a provocative gesture.

"Woman, you are special." He chuckled, looking down at her.

"I bet you're into gold prospecting, aren't you?" she asked.

"Nope."

"Cattle, then?"

"Wrong again."

"Then tell me, what sort of business appointment do you have in Montana?" she asked, frustrated that she couldn't answer correctly.

"Alice, that is your name, right?"

She nodded.

"Alice, I'm going to Montana to find the men who murdered my family, and I aim to kill them," August said, putting his hat on and tipping it towards her. "With that said, you take care of yourself, and if I ever end up in Denver again, I'll be sure to look you up." He spun around and left the room.

Aroused by his confidence and mystery, Alice called out, "Honey, you can call on me anytime."

ROSEBUD, MONTANA TERRITORY

Nell cradled Abigail in her arms while barking at Billy, "You go over to your brother's now and set him straight, you hear me?"

"I will, let me gather my things. Oh boy, when I see my baby brother, I'm gonna give him a whoopin'," Billy growled.

"You tell him that's it, the girl is comin' to live with

us," Nell barked, her nostrils flaring and eyes bulging in anger.

Abigail sat up and said, "I don't know, Aunt Nell, maybe Uncle Billy shouldn't. My dad is quite angry, and I fear he may hurt him."

"Your uncle Billy is a tough old man; he'll be fine," Nell said to Abigail before turning her ire towards Billy again. "He's your baby brother; he's eight years your junior. Go over and set him straight."

"Damn it, woman, I'm going. Let me get my boots on!" Billy grumbled.

"If you're going to move as fast as molasses in January, then I'll go," Nell said, sliding out from beside Abigail and getting to her feet. She smoothed out her dress and marched back to her bedroom. She emerged wearing a shawl and hat. "I'll be back shortly."

Billy grunted and put himself in between Nell and the front door. "You sit back down. I'm going, just takes me a bit."

"No, you don't seem able to handle that bully of a brother. I'll do it," Nell snapped and tried to push past Billy.

Standing firm, Billy said, "I'm going. I'm ready...and this time, I'll get him to understand." He looked at Abigail and winked.

"Be careful, Uncle Billy," Abigail said with concern in her voice.

Billy grabbed his coat that hung next to the front door and exited, slamming the door behind him.

Nell opened the door and cried out, "Remember, tell

him she's staying here. He's done lost his mind and lost his right to be a parent!"

"Looks like I won't have to go to his house. He's come here," Billy said, pointing down his long windy dirt drive.

Nell looked in the direction Billy was pointing and saw Evan riding their way. "Good, I'll give him a piece of my mind."

"You go inside. Lock the door," Billy ordered, his face tightening and his voice deepening.

The tone Billy spoke in just then told Nell to listen without complaint. She went back inside the house and did as he said.

Sensing the tension, Abigail asked, "What's going on?"

"It's your dad, he's here," Nell said.

Though Billy was exactly as Nell described, a tough old man, Evan was equally tough but younger and more agile. He hadn't had the rowdy and adventuresome days as a bounty hunter, but Evan didn't lack in strength or stamina.

Knowing he'd have to stand his ground and even be prepared to fight, Billy was ready and planned on telling Evan he was ready for anything through conversation and body language.

Evan rode up at a full gallop and stopped just a foot from where Billy stood in the middle of the drive. He jumped from the saddle and asked, "Where's Abigail?" He gave Billy a hard stare and continued, "You tell my daughter to come out; time for her to come home."

"Little brother, you need to listen and listen well; those days of hurting Abigail are over. Best you turn around and come back when you're prepared to give me your word that you'll never place a hand on her," Billy said.

Evan's eyes widened with anger. He marched up to within inches of Billy's face and growled, "She's my daughter, not yours." He looked past Billy and shouted, "Abigail, you come out now. Time to go home."

"You're not listening. She's not coming home with you," Billy snapped.

"You've taken a liking to my daughter, you and Nell. I get it, but know this, you have no rights, I do. She's mine not yours. Just because you couldn't have children doesn't give you some claim to mine," Evan seethed.

"You're a spiteful son of a bitch. What happened to you? You're not the boy or young man I knew all my life. You need to know that the way you're treating Abigail is not what Sally would have wanted; you and I both know that," Billy said, referencing Abigail's mother, Sally.

"Don't speak her name," Evan warned.

"She'd roll in her grave if she could see how you treat her beloved daughter. She gave her life for that girl, and every day since, you've spit on her memory," Billy said.

Evan clenched his fists and ground his jaw. The temptation to strike out was growing in him.

"You're drunk; I can smell it on you. Go home, sober up, and come back when you're prepared to be the father I know you're capable of," Billy said.

"How dare you," Evan growled.

"Go."

Done talking, Evan stepped to the side and took a step past Billy.

Not wanting their disagreement to get physical, Billy knew he couldn't allow Evan to go to the house. He put his arm out and blocked Evan. "Go home."

Inside, both Nell and Abigail were peeking outside from the front window near the door.

"I'm scared," Abigail said.

"You'll be fine. Uncle Billy, he's not going to let your dad get you," Nell said, reassuring her.

Outside, Evan craned his head to the side and snapped, "Get your hands off me."

Billy could smell the strong odor of alcohol and knew that Evan was still drunk. He shifted his tactic and tone and said, "Evan, just go. I'll stop by your house later today; we can talk more about this."

"No," Evan said, shoving Billy out of the way and continuing his march towards the house. "Come on out, Abby. Time to go home."

Seeing her father coming, Abigail looked to Nell then to her pistol lying on the table.

"It's fine. I won't let him get inside," Nell said.

"Darn it, Evan," Billy growled, knowing he'd have to escalate the confrontation. He rushed up behind Evan, grabbed him by the shoulders, and flung him back.

Evan stumbled but was able to remain standing. His anger turned to rage as he ran at Billy and tackled him to the ground.

Watching in horror, Abigail gasped when she saw her father and Billy fall to the ground and begin to wrestle.

The two men rolled around on the ground, neither getting the upper hand until Evan managed to strike Billy in the jaw with his elbow.

Dazed from the hit, Billy wasn't able to stop Evan as he climbed on top of him. Once there, Evan straddled Billy's torso and, from that advantageous position, began to pummel Billy with one punch after another.

"No!" Abigail yelped as she watched the fight turn against her uncle.

Shocked but not willing to have Billy lose, Nell turned to Abigail and said, "You stay here."

"Where are you going?" Abigail asked.

"To help," Nell said, grabbing a fire poker from the fireplace hearth and exiting the house. "You stop now!"

Abigail locked the door and rushed back to the window to watch in horror as Evan stood up from what appeared to be an unconscious Billy and approached Nell, his clenched hands bloody from the battering he'd given Billy. "You swing that at me, I'll turn it against you, Nell, I swear it," Evan yelled, pointing at the fire poker.

Nell didn't listen. She raced at Evan with the poker raised high. She swung down, but Evan grabbed it with one hand. A look of fear gripped Nell when she realized that Evan wasn't about to be defeated as easily as she thought.

Evan tore the poker from her grip and raised it above his head. "What did I tell you I was going to do?" Evan hollered.

Nell put her hands out to block what she thought was coming.

However, before he could bring the poker down, a shot rang out.

Nell flinched from the loud crack of the pistol behind her and saw the expression on Evan's face change. He looked over her shoulder towards her house. "Abby?" he asked, dropping the poker and clutching his chest.

Nell craned her head around and saw Abigail standing in the open doorway with a pistol in her trembling hands. Tears streamed down her face as she watched Evan drop to his knees.

"Abby?" Evan said, surprised that Abigail had shot him. He looked down at the wound, the blood soaking through his shirt.

Nell ran to Billy. "You okay?"

Evan pulled his hand away from his chest and gazed at his blood-covered hand. "You killed me, Ab, you killed me," he said and toppled over face-first on the ground, dead.

Abigail began to cry heavily at the sight of her now dead father. A mix of emotions ran through her; she was happy knowing he'd never hurt her again but sad at the same time. She was now officially an orphan, parentless.

"Can you get up?" Nell asked Billy, who began to stir on the ground. Nell looked back towards Abigail, who stood frozen to the same spot, the pistol now lowered to her side. "Abigail, come help me."

Snapping out of her trance, Abigail shoved the pistol

into her holster and went to Nell's side.

Seeing she was traumatized, Nell took her hand and said, "You listen here, you're gonna be fine. Your uncle Billy and me are not going to let anything happen to you. You understand that?"

Abigail nodded, but that still didn't stop her mind from going back to the dark thoughts of her hanging from a noose for the killing of her father.

"I need your help. Go to the other side of Uncle Billy and help me get him to his feet," Nell ordered.

Abigail did as she asked.

The two managed to get Billy up. He looked at the two and asked, "Where's Evan?"

Unable to answer, Abigail lowered her head in shame.

"He's gone," Nell said stoically.

"What? What happened?" Billy asked, looking around until his eyes fell on Evan's motionless body a few feet behind him.

"I shot him," Nell lied.

Stunned, Abigail stared at Nell with wide eyes.

Nell shook her head, signaling for Abigail to remain quiet.

"Why did you shoot him?" Billy asked, his speech slurred.

"'Cause I thought he'd killed you and was coming to kill us. The man was deranged, out of his mind," Nell said, taking Billy firmly by the arm. "Come, let's get you inside and clean you up."

They escorted Billy inside the house and sat him

down.

"Did you have to kill him?" Billy asked.

"Damn it, William, I had to do what I had to do. Now close your mouth so I can wash your face off," Nell scolded him, a cool wet washcloth in her hand.

Billy noticed Abigail was pacing, her gun belt hanging from her hip. "What did you shoot him with?"

Nell recoiled and snapped, "Does it matter? The drunkard is dead."

"It does to me," Billy roared, finally showing anger. He stood up and walked over to Abigail. "Let me see your pistol."

Abigail froze. She gave him a look then shifted her gaze to Nell.

"Don't look at her. Give me your pistol," Billy ordered, his hand extended.

"Leave the girl alone. Can't you see she's traumatized?" Nell barked.

Fearful that she'd done something horribly wrong, and unable to lie, she belted out, "He was going to kill Aunt Nell. I had to, Uncle Billy, I had to."

Billy's face melted into an expression of sadness and compassion. He placed his bruised hand on her shoulder and said, "I only wanted to know because you'll need my counsel on how to process such a thing."

Nell shook her head vigorously. "You just couldn't let it go."

"It's okay, Aunt Nell. I don't like to lie, especially about a thing like killing my dad."

"I know you had to, I understand that. How about

we talk later, you and I?" he asked.

She nodded.

"And, Abby, just know that it's okay for you to feel bad even though your daddy had it coming. It's a hard thing killing a person, and you should know how to process that emotion properly so you don't..." he said and paused to think.

After waiting for more than a few seconds, Abigail asked, "So you don't what?"

"So you don't enjoy it too much."

BIG CIRCLE RANCH, MILES CITY, MONTANA TERRITORY

Boyd paced in front of the packed great room of his expansive log house. Cigar smoke, loud chatter and laughter filled the space. Assembled in front of him was every man, woman and child who worked for him in some capacity. Ranch hands, maids, cooks, blacksmiths, horse handlers, you name it—if they worked for Boyd, they were there. Sitting in the front row was his son, Jed. What Jed didn't know was this last minute gathering had to do with him.

"I don't ask for much," Boyd grumbled. He ran his hand through his thick gray hair, smoothing it out before he continued. "I ask for loyalty, hard work, and honesty."

Heads began to turn slightly. They'd heard this speech before and knew it ended with someone being reprimanded. Curious, each one began to look at the others, wondering who the guilty party was.

"I'm loyal to you, I work hard for you, and I'm always honest with you," Boyd said, stopping in front of Jed. "Son, stand up."

A few mumbled loudly in the back.

Jed looked around, bewildered as to why he'd been called out to stand by his father. "Sure, what is it?" Jed asked, getting to his feet as nervousness washed over him.

"Come here, my son," Boyd said, holding out his hand and motioning Jed to come stand next to him.

Jed walked the few feet and turned around.

Boyd laid his hand on the back of his neck lightly and said, "You all know Jed. He's a hard worker, wouldn't you say?"

Many hollered out their agreement and nodded.

"You'd say he's honest, wouldn't ya?" Boyd asked.

Again the room approved.

"And no doubt you'd say he's loyal," Boyd said with a broad smile, his large mustache hiding part of it.

Once more everyone present agreed to that description of Jed.

"As of this morning, I would have agreed; then I saw this," Boyd said, holding up the wanted poster from Colton. "Someone in this room brought this to my attention, and of course, I was curious who it might be, as our little town and the county around it isn't densely populated. It's not every day, hell, we never get wanted posters hung in our town 'cause we keep this place safe; we make sure that if anyone gets out of sync or acts out, we take care of them. We don't tolerate nonsense in this town, and why? I'll tell you why, nonsense and wanted posters can hurt business."

Jed's complexion turned ashen.

"I further queried as to who this killer could be, and know what? My son's name was mentioned."

Gasps and cross chatter erupted in the room.

"Quiet!" Boyd cried out.

Instantly the room silenced.

"Upon hearing my son could be involved in a murder, I immediately challenged that, but I was told in so many words that it was true. That my son and his friend Edward—yes, you, Edward—might also be involved," Boyd said, pointing to the far corner of the room to a short man.

Edward lowered his head in a shameful manner and remained quiet.

"Edward, come on up here and stand next to Jed," Boyd said.

Sheepishly, Edward came to the front of the room and took a spot next to Jed, his head still hung low.

"Back to what I was saying. I was shocked to hear these accusations leveled at my very own son and his friend from childhood and for what? Murder. Yes, they murdered some merchant's wife. Now I've called you all here because I pledged to each and every one of you that I'd take care of you if you did the same for me. You see, we're a family, and family takes care of their own; that includes holding family members accountable," Boyd said, stepping in front of Jed and Edward.

"Jed, did you kill that woman?" Boyd asked.

"Father, it's complicated," Jed replied.

"The truth, son," Boyd asked.

"Only after she tried to kill me," Jed said.

"Edward?" Boyd asked.

"Sir, I didn't kill her, but I did stab—" Edward said.

Boyd swung and slapped Edward. "I didn't ask for excuses or explanations. I asked if you killed that woman."

"Sir, I was only helping Jed," Edward whined.

"Why?" Boyd asked both men.

"That savage...she did me wrong. A few months back she pulled a gun on me and threatened to kill me. She humiliated me, and I swore I'd get my family honor back," Jed complained.

"Family honor? Why did she pull a gun on you? Where did this happen?"

"At her cabin a few miles north of town. Me and Edward were riding by when she enticed us, she used her native siren song to lure us in, but when we stopped by, she turned on us," Jed replied.

"You go to her house, you step foot on her land, she pulls a gun on you and orders you to leave?" Boyd asked, trying to understand correctly what happened.

"Not exactly like that but close," Jed answered.

Boyd's eyes widened with anger. He stepped forward until the tip of his nose was almost touching Jed's. "Please enlighten us all."

"Edward said she waved for us to come over in a seductive way," Jed said.

"I didn't say that," Edward cried out.

"Yes, you did," Jed snapped.

"No, I didn't," Edward fired back. The two men yelled at each other a few times.

"Both of you shut up!" Boyd roared.

The men grew quiet.

"I don't care what you think she did or didn't do. You went onto someone else's land, and they ran you off; but somehow you feel entitled, you feel like you deserve to trespass, and when you get turned away, you go and murder and call it redeeming honor!"

"It's not that simple," Jed said.

Boyd cocked back his arm and again slapped Jed. "Shut your damn mouth. Do you not know how long I've worked to get us to where we are? How long I've lobbied in the territorial capital? Soon we'll be a state, and when that happens, I hope to leverage my influence to better us all. Hell, I might even become one of the first senators from Montana, but I can't if my family name is ruined by my damn fool son."

"I'm sorry, Father," Jed groaned.

"If you weren't my son...or his lifelong friend, I'd take you both out and string you up from that old bur oak out front. No, what I'm going to do is punish you and leave it at that, and here's why; we're family, all of us, all of you seated here. I could have punished these two in private, but I chose to be transparent with everyone here because family talks and family opens up. If we're all to succeed, we need to look out for each other."

"What are you going to do to us?" Jed asked.

Boyd turned to his right-hand man, Clement, and said, "Take these two out back and give them ten lashes each."

Clement, a close friend and associate of Boyd's for over forty years, stepped forward. He nodded to Boyd and walked up to Jed and Edward. "Come on, you two."

A terrified look gripped both of their faces with Jed crying out, "Father, please don't do this."

Boyd came at Jed with anger in his step. He took Jed by the jaw with his meaty hands and snapped, "You're lucky someone here doesn't turn you in." He turned to the group gathered and barked, "I know rumors are out there, and after today that stops. No one will utter a word about the murder of that Indian nor anything about these two. Does everyone understand?"

Everyone nodded; some cried out, "Yes."

"If I hear one word, one simple thing that says anyone said something, I'll kill you. Do I make myself clear?"

Again the group nodded with some verbally acknowledging.

"We're family. We help each other; we have each other's backs, including lying to protect the other. I know there's a sizable bounty and you might be thinking you could easily cash in and ride off; but know I'll find out, and I'll spend every dollar to track you down. I'll put a bounty out for your head that will exceed what you'll get. I'll make sure that bounty for your head is so high that every bounty hunter west of the Mississippi comes looking for you."

Fear gripped the faces of those seated there because they knew Boyd never exaggerated.

"Pop, please don't do this!" Jed pleaded as Clement escorted them out the back.

"Sorry, son, time for you to suffer the consequences of your actions. Just be grateful you're not hanging from that tree or some gallows in town," Boyd replied to Jed.

Clement, along with two other men, tied both Jed and Edward to a fence off one of the small outbuildings.

One by one, the group that had gathered inside made their way out and circled around to watch.

Jed cried out, but his pleas fell on deaf ears.

Edward remained stoic as if he was accepting of the punishment.

Clement ripped the shirts off the men's backs, readied a horse whip, and looked to Boyd for approval to start.

Boyd called out, "These two men, our family members, lied to us. They risked all of us by going out and making an unsanctioned killing. They'll now suffer our justice, and when this is over, it is over; we shall never speak of it again."

No one uttered a word. The silence from the group was eerie.

Boyd looked at Clement and nodded.

With the approval granted, Clement raised the horse whip and brought the first strike down against Jed's back.

Jed yelped and cried out, "No, Father, please."

"Take it like a man, Jed!" Boyd barked. He was embarrassed by Jed's public display.

Clement reared back and again brought the whip against Jed. In slow repetition, he did it eight more times.

When he was done; Jed's back was mostly red and swollen with welts except for two areas where the whip had broken the skin.

"Cut him down," Boyd ordered.

Two men stepped forward and sliced the rope that was now holding Jed up, as he'd passed out from the pain.

Free from the bindings, Jed fell to the ground unconscious.

"Take him to his room and clean him up," Boyd ordered. He gave Clement another look and said, "Proceed with Edward."

Not hesitating, Clement began delivering the lashes to Edward, who stood erect and firm, taking each hit with hardly a grimace of pain on his face. When Clement was done, he tossed the whip aside and cut Edward free himself. "Go to the bunkhouse and wash up."

Edward nodded and sauntered off, his stride lessened and his pace slower than normal.

Taking a spot in front of the group, Boyd closed the gathering. "We all witnessed the justice given to those family members of ours. Like I said before, it is over; never will we speak of this again. Go back to your responsibilities; focus on that, nothing more."

Everyone walked off in different directions.

Clement approached Boyd and said, "Whipping Jed was one of the hardest things I've ever done; I consider him like a son."

Boyd patted Clement's shoulder and said, "The boy needed it, and justice for our family had to be done.

Thank you for administering it."

"You're welcome."

Boyd leaned in and whispered, "Have your two best men keep tabs on everyone. I need to know if anyone does plan on outing Jed and Edward for the bounty."

"Already on it, boss."

"Good man," Boyd said. "And tell me the second you hear anything. I won't tolerate that nor give any mercy. If someone crosses me, no quarter; they're to be put under house arrest until I deal with them."

"Yes, boss."

"Now then, let's get back to the business of Big Circle," Boyd said and walked off towards the main house.

ROCKLAND, IDAHO TERRITORY

Margaret placed the steaming plate of potatoes and roast beef in front of Grant and said, "I made your favorite tonight."

Grant raised his brow, shocked to see the roast. "What's the occasion?"

"Who cares?" George said, diving in with his fork and knife.

Grant slapped George's hand and said, "We say grace and give thanks first. You know better."

"Sorry, Pa," George said.

The three locked hands and prayed. When they were done, Grant again asked, "It's not Sunday or my birthday or a holiday, so why the roast?"

"I felt like it. You gave me authority in the household, and I thought today was a good day to have roast," Margaret replied, cutting into the slab in front of her.

"But we only have so much," Grant said, holding his utensils in his hands.

"I know that. Why can't I just serve my family a good meal? We've finished the second day of harvest, the crop yielded well, and I wanted to have something nice, something special," Margaret said, defending her decision to serve the red meat.

Seeing she was getting defensive, Grant backed off and said, "You're right."

"Enjoy," Margaret said.

"Thank you, Margaret. You're a good young lady and a wonderful cook," Grant said, taking a bite of the roast and savoring it.

"I learned from the best," Margaret said, referring to her mother.

"She was," Grant said, his thoughts slipping to his wife. He looked at the opposite end of the table, where she used to sit, and stared.

"It's not the same without her," Margaret said, now looking down at the empty seat.

"I miss her singing," George said sadly.

"Oh, her voice, it was so sweet, prettier than any of the angels in heaven," Grant said with a big smile.

Margaret grew silent and lowered her head.

Noticing Margaret, Grant asked, "What is it?"

"It's nothing," Margaret answered, pushing food

around on her plate.

Grant reached out and touched her hand. "I tried everything I could that day."

"It's not that," Margaret said, looking up from her plate. "I know you did everything you could to save her."

Grant nodded, a frown appearing on his face.

"Pa, after Mama died, you told me and George that you'd never lie to us," Margaret said.

Grant thought and said, "You're right, I said that. Why are you bringing that up now?"

"You kept Mama's illness from us until it was too late. I wish I would have known earlier so I could be with her, tell her every day how I loved her," Margaret said, tears welling in her eyes.

Suddenly Grant knew where this was going.

"Today in your bedroom, I found this," Margaret said in a trembling voice as she placed the bloody handkerchief on the table.

Grant and George both stared at it.

"Is that yours, Pa?" George asked.

Not wanting to see it any longer, Grant swiped it from the table and pocketed it. "I cut myself is all."

"Pa, you're lying," Margaret said, wiping tears from her eyes.

Torn between a desire to protect his children from the truth and the responsibility to honor his word, he sided with the latter. "I am lying. I have something wrong with me. Not quite sure what it is, but I've had a bad cough. Yesterday I coughed up a bunch of blood."

"Are you dying?" George asked, his mouth wide

open in shock.

"No," Grant quickly replied, though he sensed his ailment was very bad.

"I want Doc Warren to come check you out," Margaret insisted.

"I don't have time for Doc Warren. We've got four acres still to harvest—"

Cutting him off, Margaret snapped, "You also promised you'd take care of yourself, remember?"

Knowing she was right, Grant nodded. "You're right, I said that."

"Then it's settled. I'm going to go get Doc tomorrow and bring him back here."

"Very well," Grant said. He looked at her then turned his gaze to a worried-looking George. "Can we now finish this fine meal and change the topic?"

Margaret touched his hand gently and said, "Let's do that and, Pa, thank you."

"You're welcome, sweetheart."

ROSEBUD, MONTANA TERRITORY

After they had buried Evan's body behind the barn, Billy and Abigail went for a walk in the far field so they could have their talk.

The sun was beginning to set, casting their shadows long and coloring the surrounding hills in an orange glow.

"Why don't we go tell the marshal what happened?" Abigail asked.

"'Cause we don't need the law messing things up.

You did what was right, and we'll leave it at that," Billy replied.

"So they might arrest me and hang me?" Abigail asked, a tinge of fear in her voice.

"Now, now, ain't no one going to arrest you, and there's not a chance in hell you're going to hang. No one will ever know, and makes no sense to tell anyone. This was a private matter."

"Won't someone come looking for him?" Abigail asked, fearing a full-scale investigation would be launched.

"Who is going to come looking for your drunkard of a father?" Billy said, stating what Abigail knew was the truth. Evan was known as the area drunk; he didn't have any friends and didn't work except for doing day-laborer work now and then to make enough money to buy booze.

"So that's it?" Abigail asked, confused that she could kill a man, her father, and nothing would happen.

"It's our family secret," Billy said, draping his arm over her shoulder and hugging her tight. "Speaking of what happened, how do you feel about killing your dad?" Billy asked, not at all concerned about the sensitivity of the topic.

"To be honest, I have mixed feelings. On one hand, I'm glad he's dead. My dad was a mean and despicable person. I never knew him to love or nurture me; but on the other hand, I'm now all alone," Abigail answered, her hand extended to feel the tall grasses just beside her.

Billy took her arm and turned her to face him. "You're never alone with me and Aunt Nell; we're family and we'll take care of you."

"I know that, but knowing the two people who created me are gone, dead, is an odd feeling," Abigail said.

"I get that, but please know you're not alone," Billy said.

"Is it wrong for me not to feel guilty for killing him?" Abigail asked.

"You feel nothing?"

"No, I do, but I don't feel guilt. I felt guilt when I stole candy from the general store when I was eight only to bring it back the next day; but this, I don't. Is something wrong with me?" she asked.

"What do you feel?" he asked.

"I wasn't sure I could do it. I saw what he'd done to you, and then Aunt Nell went to confront him. When I saw he'd taken the fire poker away from her and was about to hit her with it, I just reacted. I couldn't let someone like him, a bad man, hurt someone I loved. After I shot him, a jolt of fear coursed through me."

"Hmm," Billy said, nodding. He understood the feeling and was glad he could talk her through it. "Go on."

"I knew the gun was a powerful thing, meaning I knew it had the power to kill, but I'd only ever thought about it, fantasized it even; but after I squeezed that trigger, a sense of that power entered me."

"So no regrets?"

"None whatsoever. If I had to do it all over again, I would."

"So you'd have no problem killing again?" Billy

asked, genuinely curious.

She turned away and kept walking.

He caught up and asked, "Do you think you could do it again?"

"How do I answer without sounding like a killer? I'm not a killer. It's not my intent, nor my desire, to murder or kill people, but if I had to wield a weapon again to defend the defenseless, I would."

"So only to kill to protect the innocent?"

"Yes, exactly."

"And no remorse for killing your own father?" Billy asked.

"None, he was my father because he helped make me, but he isn't my dad in the sense that he loved me and showed me how to be a good person or gave me values. You did that, Uncle Billy," she said.

A tear welled in Billy's eye. "Girl, that's the nicest thing I've ever had someone say to me."

"It's true. You and Aunt Nell are my real parents, not that Mama couldn't have been, God didn't give her a chance to be."

"Can you share what you just told me with Aunt Nell?" Billy asked.

"Of course," she said. The two stopped and stared as the sun dipped below the far horizon. A long pause separated their conversation until she asked, "How old were you when you killed your first man?"

"Thirty-four, I was in Wichita. Me and Tillis were hunting one of the meanest hombres I'd ever come across. By then Tillis had killed thirteen men, I believe.

He was a killing machine. I think he enjoyed it, and it was also practical in his mind. When the wanted poster said *dead or alive*, he thought it best to bring them in dead—made it easier and you never have to worry about a dead man."

"When you say he enjoyed it, do you mean he took joy in ending people's lives?" Abigail asked.

"Let me phrase it this way, he didn't run around killing women and children, although he did put a round in this one split tail outside Dodge City; she was defending her man, a road agent that we'd caught up to. She was slinging lead at us and he gave her the chance to surrender. When she responded with more lead, he placed one right there," Billy said, placing his index finger on his forehead.

"He killed a woman?"

"A bad woman. Anyway, I digressed. Let me clarify ole Abraham Tillis, he enjoyed taking out the trash, as he put it. If you were a bad man, he'd have no problem putting a well-placed round in ya."

She nodded.

"You understand the difference?" Billy asked.

"I do. He killed bad men."

"Yep. Thing is old Tillis was built for killing bad men. He believed that the only way to fight the violence of a bad men was for good men to exercise equal or greater violence against them."

"I agree with that," she said.

Billy smiled and leaned in. "Don't tell that to your aunt Nell. She'll think I've corrupted your mind."

"So what happened?"

"With what? Oh, yeah, the first man I killed? We closed in on William Maxwell; he was holed up in a brothel. I volunteered to go fetch him in his room while Tillis stood in the hallway. Just before going into the room, the whore came out, spooking us both. She told me Maxwell was taking a bath and that his gun belt was on the bed. I knew I had him, so I went in and declared myself and that I was going to arrest him. Well, I failed right there. Don't run your mouth; just go in and get it done. Anyway, his gun belt was on the bed, but his Scofield pistol was sitting next to him on a stool. He grabbed it and took a shot at me. Damn bullet went through my hat, just barely missing the top of my head. I shot him right in the tub, put a bullet into his chest and another in his neck. Boy, I was shaking; my entire body felt like it was vibrating. I had assumed it was easy and he wasn't armed, and I almost lost my life."

"How did you feel after that?"

"A bit odd, I kept seeing his face, the expression on it. He was a serious man, he wasn't scared at all, and if he hadn't given me a haircut with that shot or had the chance to shoot another, I wouldn't be talking to you right now. You gotta know that some men are deliberate, they won't wait, and they'll kill you without a second's thought, not even ask a question. Those men, it's best you kill them first."

"Understood."

"Fortunately for me I was a quick study. Never made that mistake again."

"You said Tillis is now living in Idaho? He retired?" Abigail asked.

"Like I said, last I heard. He changed his name, met a fine woman, she gave him religion, and now he's growing potatoes." Billy laughed.

"Strange," Abigail mused.

"What's strange about it?"

"That a notorious bounty hunter like him would now be a potato farmer. Why not keep doing what you're good at?"

"'Cause people change, Abby. It's okay to change your ways or your thoughts. It's called growing."

"Well, I think your life running with Tillis sounds romantic. I want to be a bounty hunter," Abigail said, gleaming.

"Being a gunman or bounty hunting isn't for young ladies. I don't mind you learning how to defend yourself like you did earlier, but hunting bad men for money is a man's job," Billy said.

Abigail fretted and asked, "Who said that?"

"It's just the way it is, period. Don't go thinking you can do that. Get that out of your mind."

Abigail didn't reply, she simply smiled and thought to herself that soon she'd be eighteen and be able to go do whatever her heart desired.

CHAPTER THREE

ROCKLAND, IDAHO TERRITORY

AUGUST 23, 1888

Grant dug his hand into the moist fresh-tilled earth and pulled out two large potatoes. He brushed off the caked-on soil and held them proudly in his hand. He didn't much like farming but appreciated the result of so much hard work. Looking out, he saw George working the earth and pulling up handfuls of potatoes and placing them in a basket that was strapped to the side of a mule. He wanted more for him, but George was a different person than him; he'd never experience the life he had, nor did he seem to have any desire for adventure. Grant had never mentioned his past to his children and planned on keeping it that way. He had wondered if his genes would show up in his children, and the closest he saw of him was in Margaret. She was determined, headstrong and fearless. He wasn't sure what was going to happen to them after he died, and that fear was possibly becoming a reality. After Margaret had ridden into town to get the doctor, he'd had another coughing fit, which resulted in him spitting up copious amounts of thick red bloody phlegm.

While the farm made a small profit, it wasn't enough to ensure his children would be fine. He needed to secure more land so they could grow more, and in order to do that he needed more money. He wouldn't be worried, as he had been saving, but now that he knew he was sick, he felt time was running out.

"No daydreaming!" George hollered from afar.

Jolted back to the present, Grant went back to work only to be distracted when he heard the heavy galloping of a couple of horses. He stood up straight and looked towards the road to see two horsemen coming towards his house. Hoping it had nothing to do with Margaret, he rushed to meet them.

Walking up to the two men, he asked, "How can I help you, gentlemen?"

"Grant Toomey?" one man asked, leaning forward on his pommel enough so that his badge popped out from underneath his jacket.

"Who's looking for him?" Grant asked.

"United States Marshal Cussler."

"Is there some sort of trouble?" Grant asked, his instincts kicking in as he began to size up both men.

"No trouble. Are you Mr. Toomey?"

"I am."

"We've come to serve you notice that a lien has been placed against your property," Cussler said, pulling a folded piece of paper from his inside jacket pocket and handing it to Grant.

Grant took the paper and unfolded it. As he read, Cussler explained, "Apparently you never paid the federal transfer fee that was established by the Territorial Commission."

"What transfer fee?" Grant asked, folding the paper

up and giving the marshal a hard stare.

"I don't make the laws, Mr. Toomey, I simply enforce them; but my understanding is when you staked the claim sixteen years ago, you were supposed to pay a transfer fee to the Territorial Commission in the amount of one hundred dollars back then, but didn't."

"I don't know anything about that, but if it's money you need, let me go get that hundred dollars and be done with this business," Grant said.

"I'm afraid it's not that simple. The fee was supposed to have been paid within six months of you occupying your claim from the territorial government. You'll need to go to the territorial capital in Boise and make the payment plus fines. You have two months to do that."

"Fine? How much is it?" Grant asked.

Cussler gave his deputy a look and shook his head. It was apparent he disliked this part of his job. "It's seven hundred dollars."

"I don't have that kind of money. I'm a potato farmer," Grant snapped, his anger rising.

"Mr. Toomey, my heart goes out to ya, it does. I suggest you get that payment to Boise before the sixty-day mark so you can keep your farm," Cussler said.

"I'm gonna have to sell. There's no way I can come up with that sort of money," Grant barked.

"What you do to get that money is none of my business. Now if you don't have further questions, I'll leave you to get back to your work," Cussler said, tipping his hat and turning his horse around.

Grant watched as the two men rode off. He

unfolded the paper again, and as he reread it, his anger swelled until he exploded into a fit of rage. He crumpled the paper in his fist and threw it on the ground. Seeing a wooden box close by, he stormed over and kicked it hard enough to shatter it.

From across the field, George saw Grant acting out and ran over. "Pa, what's wrong?"

"The damn government bureaucrats have figured out a way to take our land," Grant barked.

"I don't understand," George said.

"If I don't find a way to pay the Idaho Territorial government seven hundred dollars within sixty days, we lose the farm."

"What?" George said, stunned, his face turning ashen.

"I should ride into Boise and shoot them, that's what I should do," Grant bellowed loudly.

"Pa, calm down. We'll figure this out," George said calmly. He walked over to Grant and placed his hand on his shoulder. "We're the Toomeys, we always find a way; plus you've never shot a man in your life, would you even know how?"

Grant felt an urge for a brief second to declare how he'd have no problem shooting them in Boise 'cause he was a killer, but quickly dashed the idea, instead choosing to listen to George and calm down. He looked fondly upon his wise son and said, "You're right. We will figure this out."

"We always find a way. Remember a few years back when the well ran dry?" George asked.

"I do."

"What happened?"

"We found a way," Grant replied, his temper melting away.

George picked up the crumpled paper and pocketed it. We have to pay it off no matter if we get angry or not; it's gotta be done."

"How did you get to become so wise?" Grant asked, astonished at his son's levelheaded response.

"I'm assuming from Mother," George quipped with a wink.

Grant felt a coughing fit coming on, so he said, "You go back to work. I need to use the outhouse."

"Listen, Pa, we'll be fine if we do it as a family," George said, patting Grant on the shoulder, and ran back to his place in the field.

Not wanting George to see him cough, Grant rushed to the outhouse and began to hack violently until he spit out a large amount of blood. As his mind swam with all the different scenarios, he longed for what he considered the simpler days of hunting bad men for large bounties. He didn't have complicated taxes or fees to deal with. It was a matter of tracking down the target, getting them, and taking a stack of cash upon delivery. What could he do? How could he come up with seven hundred dollars in sixty days? He had some money saved but nothing close to that amount. As his anger again began to rise, George's voice popped in his head and calmed him down. George was right, they could find a way, but in order to figure it out, he needed to keep his wits about him.

ROSEBUD, MONTANA TERRITORY

Billy slowly mounted the wagon, grunting when he sat down on the hard wooden seat. "My body aches."

"Of course it does, you should be resting not going into town. You just got beat up yesterday," Nell said, shaking her head in disagreement with his plan to go for supplies. Grumbling under her breath, she walked back inside the house.

Abigail practically leapt into the seat. The expression on her face was telling; a grin stretched from ear to ear and her eyes were sparkling.

Billy looked at her and asked, "You sure you want to come with me to Miles City?"

"I've never been. Of course I want to go," Abigail replied happily.

Nell emerged from the house with food wrapped in two towels. She placed both in the wagon just behind the seat. "There's bread, jam and some bacon; should be enough to see you through the trip."

"Thank you, darlin'," Billy said, giving Nell a flirtatious wink.

Seeing Billy, Nell smacked him on the leg and said, "You focus on taking care of our girl, you hear?"

"I will, don't you worry," Billy said.

"I'll be fine, Aunt Nell," Abigail said, placing her right hand on the back strap of her Colt.

"And you had to wear trousers? You couldn't go into town looking presentable?" Nell complained.

"I feel more comfortable this way," Abigail said.

Nell rolled her eyes and walked off. "I'll expect you two back by mid-evening. Ride safe."

"Goodbye, sweetheart," Billy said, flicking the reins of his horse.

"Be safe, and don't be gone too long," Nell said, waving as they pulled away and slowly disappeared over the rolling hills.

MILES CITY, MONTANA TERRITORY

Abigail enjoyed the ride. Being outside and going somewhere for longer than the short ride from her house to Uncle Billy's was a treat in and of itself. To be able to ride to the bigger town of Miles City was thrilling. As they rode into town, her eyes were wide and took in all the sights and storefronts. Back and forth her head snapped, her mind taking mental snapshots of everything. Her mind asked endless questions about what was inside each store or place of business. She then questioned if they'd stop by the local saloon or bar and get a drink. Whatever it was, it was all new for her and exciting.

As planned, they stopped at the mercantile store. Inside, she marveled at everything on the shelves; it had been so long since she'd been to a town like Miles City, much less to a store, that she was in awe.

"If you drop or break anything, you buy it," the clerk at the front cried out when he saw Abigail fondling a magnifying glass.

"Are you talking to me?" Abigail asked, pointing to herself.

"Yes, you," the clerk said.

Billy walked up to her and said, "Just put it down. These people are stuffy."

"I didn't mean any harm," Abigail said, putting the magnifying glass softly back on the shelf.

"Here you go," Billy said to the clerk, giving him a note, which listed all the supplies they needed. He looked back over his shoulder to find Abigail now fondling a compass.

The clerk saw and rolled his eyes. "Miss, please."

"Listen, friend, she's not hurting anything. If she breaks it, I'll buy it; now leave her be," Billy snapped.

The clerk nodded and went back to fulfilling Billy's order.

Abigail smiled at Billy and went back to what she was doing. Out of the corner of her eye on the far wall at the back of the store, she spotted something curious. She walked back and noticed it was a wanted poster. She read it, and when she got to the bottom, her eyes widened. "Seven thousand dollars?" She ripped it off the wall and rushed up to Billy. "Look, Uncle Billy."

At first he ignored her, his full attention on the clerk, ensuring his order was properly handled.

"They're paying seven thousand dollars," Abigail said with a thrill in her voice.

Hearing the large amount, Billy snapped his head and said, "Let me see that." Like her, his eyes widened when he read the bounty amount.

"It sounds like a lot, is it really?" Abigail asked.

"Oh, it's a lot, it certainly is," Billy said, holding the

poster up to the clerk, and asked, "What do you know about this?"

"Colton the Indian lover's wife was murdered. He's trying to find the killer," the clerk snarked.

"Indian lover?" Abigail asked.

"He married a Cheyenne. She was found murdered recently. Some say it was her family from the reservation; others say it was someone from the Big Circle Ranch. Thing is, if it was someone from the ranch, they'll never get taken in."

"Why's that?" Billy asked.

"On account that the name being floated as the killer is the ranch owner's son, that's why," the clerk answered.

Billy was intrigued by the thought of going out on the hunt again, especially for a job that was this close to home, but quickly brushed it aside. He handed the poster back to Abigail, who stood behind him like a puppy ready to play. He finished his business with the clerk and proceeded outside with Abigail in tow.

"What do you think, Uncle Billy?" Abigail asked, her eyes fixed on the poster.

"Think about what?" Billy asked as he tied down the supplies in the back of the wagon.

"This wanted poster, its right here in town; the killers are here, most likely at that ranch, the Big Circle Ranch," she said, hardly taking a breath.

He stopped what he was doing and looked at her. "Are you suggesting I do a job?"

"Noooo, I'm suggesting WE do a job."

He laughed heartedly and said, "My sweet girl, if I

were to even think about taking that job, I wouldn't take you with me. Your aunt Nell would kill me every which way she could imagine."

"Maybe she doesn't have to know. We could tell her we're going out to hunt or shoot or whatever. You could show me how to be a bounty hunter," she said, walking up next to him, her pleading eyes fixed on him.

"No."

"Please, this could be something special for us."

"This isn't like going out for a hunt or fishin'. This is dangerous stuff you're talking about. You have fantasies because I've told you fanciful stories, but many men try to do what I did and ended up dead. This isn't a game," he grumbled.

"I'm not a child anymore. I killed my first man yesterday, and I can handle a gun," she countered.

He looked around, hoping no one overheard, and pulled her close. Just above a whisper, he chided her, "You keep what happened yesterday to yourself, you hear? That too was serious stuff, grown-up stuff. Yes, you did what you did, but you had to. This is different; this is a choice."

She folded her arms in protest and stared at him.

"You can give me those looks all you want, but the answer is no. Now would you like to go get some candy or a root beer down at the Elk's Head Saloon before we go?"

"You're treating me like a child," she fumed.

"No, I'm not. Personally, I like candy and root beer. Your aunt Nell tells me all the time I have a sweet tooth," he quipped, hoping to steer the conversation away from the bounty.

Abigail didn't reply; she stood her ground, arms still crossed.

Seeing she needed more persuasion, he placed both hands on her shoulders and said, "Abby, I'll make you a bargain. I'll teach you more shooting skills, like riding and shooting and how to fan your Colt, but I won't take you on a dangerous job like that. Plus, we don't even know whom we'd be looking for. This is harder than most jobs. First we have to find who the killer actually is then go find them."

"I can help, I'm smart, and being a girl, I can infiltrate and get information where an old man like yourself couldn't."

She was right, being a woman could be beneficial for a job like this to gather information, but never in a million years would he put her into that situation. "No."

"I'll do it myself," Abigail growled.

"No, you won't, and if I find out you try to, there will be hell to pay."

She lowered her head and pouted.

"C'mon, sweetheart, let's go have some fun then head home. Aunt Nell will be fuming if we're late; plus I hear she's making potato pancakes and ribs for dinner."

She thought about everything he said and came to the realization he was right. She had let her youthful enthusiasm get away from her. "Okay, let's go get some root beer first."

"That sounds like a plan."

"Can we bring a jug of it home for later and to share with Aunt Nell?" Abigail said.

"Of course," he said, draping his arm over her shoulder and escorting her down the street to the Elk's Head Saloon.

Wanting to keep the poster as a sort of memento, she shoved it into her pocket.

ROCKLAND, IDAHO TERRITORY

"Take a deep breath, hold it, and exhale," Doc Warren said, a stethoscope pressed to Grant's back.

Grant did as he said, with each deep inhale bringing him discomfort.

"Again," Doc said, moving the head of the stethoscope to another point on his back.

"Do you hear anything?" Grant asked.

"Ssh," Doc scolded. "Deep breath and hold."

Grant listened and did as he was told without saying anything else. He made sure to have the examination done in the privacy of his bedroom against the wishes of Margaret, who feared he'd again lie about his condition. Grant had told her he'd have to get naked and thought that was inappropriate but promised to share what the doctor told him.

Doc removed the stethoscope and placed it back into his black leather case, walked around, and stood in front of Grant. "Lie down on the bed."

Grant did as he said, feeling awkward and uncomfortable.

Doc began to press around his torso. He pressed deep in one area and asked, "Does that hurt?"

"No."

He shifted and did the same thing. "What about here?"

"No."

"Here?"

"No."

Doc stood up and said, "How long you been coughing?"

"Four, maybe five weeks," Grant answered, sitting up.

"Blood?"

"Yes, started a few days ago."

"A lot?"

"Yes."

"Is it dark red blood or blackish?"

"Dark red."

"Hmm, okay, you can put your shirt back on," Doc ordered, walking back to his black bag and closing it with a snap.

"What is it? What's wrong with me?"

"Mr. Toomey, I believe you have lung disease. Were you ever a miner?"

"Lung disease?" Grant asked, shocked yet not too surprised by the diagnosis.

"The only real way to know is exploratory surgery, but I don't believe you'd want that. So were you?"

"What?"

"A miner? I ask because a large percentage of miners

up end with black lung, but mainly the issue they complain of is difficulty breathing. The coughing up of blood is more a symptom of lung disease, not black lung."

"No, I wasn't a miner."

"Smoke a lot?" Doc asked.

"Now and then, but never really smoked. I don't like the taste," Grant confessed.

"Without cutting you open and based upon your symptoms of being fatigued, coughing up blood and general discomfort, I have to say you have lung disease."

"Is there a cure?"

"I'm afraid not," Doc said.

"How long do I have?"

After washing his hands in a basin on the chest of drawers, Doc turned and answered him while toweling off his hands, "Could be two months, could be six; heck I've heard of some people lasting a year. I recommend you go to a sanitarium for treatment; they can ease your pain and let you live a bit longer."

"I'm not going to any sanitarium," Grant grumbled. He'd heard enough. He shot to his feet and headed for the door.

"How would you like to handle payment?" Doc asked.

Grant opened the door, but before stepping out, he asked, "How much?"

"Ten dollars for the visit and examination," Doc replied after slipping on his jacket.

"I'll pay you in cash. Meet me in the front room,"

Grant said and walked out. As he strode past the kitchen on his way to the front room, Margaret saw him and sprang to her feet.

"What did he say?" she asked.

Ignoring her, Grant opened the secretary and pulled out an envelope. He removed a single bill and put the envelope back. When he closed the secretary, he locked it with an old skeleton key.

Doc appeared and held out his hand.

"There you go, Doc, and thank you for coming out," Grant said.

"If you change your mind about the sanitarium—"

"That will be enough," Grant snapped loudly, cutting Doc off.

Taking the hint, Doc nodded and promptly exited the house.

"Sanitarium? For what? Pa, tell me, you promised," Margaret pleaded.

George came into the room and asked, "What did Doc have to say?"

Grant gritted his teeth. Just the thought he'd have to tell his children he was dying was almost unbearable. Here he was now threatened with losing his farm, and now it was all but confirmed he was going to die soon.

Margaret stepped forward and took Grant's hand. "Pa, tell us, please," she said with a tender voice.

"I want you two to sit down," Grant said, pointing to the love seat along the back wall.

Doing what he said without question, they sat and pensively waited for what they suspected was dreadful news.

Margaret's eyes had already welled up with tears with anticipation of news that would emotionally destroy her.

"I...um...darn, I just don't know how to say it. Hmm, how do I say it?" Grant said, struggling.

"It's okay, Pa. We can handle whatever you need to tell us," George said, his head held high in an attempt to remain strong for Margaret and to prove to Grant he was becoming a man.

Tears now welled in Grant's eyes. He wiped them away and said, "It's lung disease. I have lung disease."

"You're dying?" Margaret bellowed.

"Yes, I'm dying," Grant confirmed.

Margaret burst out crying.

George put his arm around her and started to comfort her.

"Doc says I have a little while or maybe upwards of a year; but I'll be honest, I think that's too optimistic."

"Is there any sort of treatment?" George asked.

"He said I could go to a sanitarium in Colorado, but I'm not leaving the farm. We've worked too hard to make this successful for me to up and leave. And we need to find a way to pay the territorial government back. I don't have the luxury of time nor the resources to go to Colorado."

"If it will save your life, you must go," Margaret wailed.

Grant stepped over and knelt in front of her. He took her hands in his and said, "My dear, sweet Margaret. Going to Colorado isn't about curing me, it's a place to go and die."

Margaret wrapped her arms around him and buried her head in his chest. "Oh, Pa, you can't die. We need you."

George hugged the two of them and began to softly cry.

He kissed them both on the top of their heads and said, "I love you two. You're the greatest gift a man could ever receive."

MILES CITY, MONTANA TERRITORY

"How's your root beer?" Billy asked a smiling Abigail.

"It's sooo good," she replied, taking another big gulp of the foaming concoction.

The bartender stepped over and said, "You two want another round?"

Billy cocked his head and asked, "What do you say, how about one more?"

Abigail lifted her head from the mug and said with beaming eyes, "Yes, please."

"I'll be right back," the bartender said, walking off.

The Elk's Head was busy, and the sound of booming laughter, talking, and poker chips could be heard all around them.

When not focused on her drink, she'd look around the bar, taking in the foreign scenery of the establishment. At a table just behind them, six men were playing poker. She watched for a second then asked, "Do you play?"

Billy craned his head back and replied, "Not

anymore; I lost my limit for life many years back."

"You're not any good?" she asked.

"That's exactly it. I'm not any good, and it took me many years and a ton of lost cash to finally admit that to myself," Billy confided jokingly.

"Can you teach me?"

"I don't think you want me teaching you. Best you learn from someone who knows how to play and win," Billy said.

Three men stepped up to the bar to the right of Billy and ordered a drink. Billy didn't pay them too much attention until he overheard them talking about the murder and the wanted poster.

"I know what Boyd said, but that cash bounty is huge. If I had that, I could finally head to Seattle and start that fishing business," one of the men, whose name was Bart, said.

"Don't be a damn fool, Bart. If Boyd even heard you saying such things, he'd tie you to that tree and whip ya," the man next to Bart said.

Bart snapped his head, glared at the man, and asked, "He'd only know I said anything if you opened your mouth. And why do you care? We could split the bounty."

"I don't want anything to do with that," the second man said, pushing away from the bar and heading towards the exit.

Bart shouted, "Don't leave. C'mon, we just got here."

The third man remained quiet, taking small sips of

his whiskey.

"What do you think?" Bart asked the third man.

"I think if you're going to do anything, you do it right; but also know the consequences could be high if you're caught by Boyd," the third man replied.

"So you're interested?" Bart asked.

"Of course I'm interested, but would I ever dare try? Not just no, but hell no. Boyd won't just tie you to the tree and whip you; I think if you or anyone outed his boy, Jed, he'd have you killed."

"Not if I plan it right, collect the bounty, and head west immediately. What do you say, Thaddeus?" Bart asked.

"Count me out," Thaddeus answered finally, tossing back the shot glass of whiskey with a final gulp and slamming it on the top of the bar. "One more pour."

The bartender nodded but was busy setting the drinks down in front of Abigail and Billy.

"If Aunt Nell saw me, she'd cry foul," Abigail said happily, taking her fresh root beer. She licked the foam off the top and took a big swallow.

Billy didn't reply to her; his attention was on the back-and-forth with the two men.

"Uncle Billy, are you listening?" Abigail asked after noticing he was focused on something else.

"Oh…sorry, what is it?" Billy asked.

"Aunt Nell, we can't tell her about my second mug," Abigail said.

"Yes, you're right, we can't," Billy confirmed and immediately went back to eavesdropping on the men.

"What are you doing?" Abigail asked.

Billy leaned up close to her and whispered, "I'm gathering information from listening to conversations."

"You are?" Abigail asked, intrigued.

"If you just sit and listen, you'll be surprised what you hear," Billy answered.

Abigail looked past Billy and saw the two men. She leaned and picked up a few words concerning what they were saying. "Are they talking about the murder of that Indian woman?"

"Sshh," Billy said.

Not wanting to interrupt Billy, she stopped talking.

With Abigail now quiet, Billy went back to listening to the two men.

Thaddeus took his second glass of whiskey, but this time he didn't sip; he poured it quickly down his throat.

"Get another," Bart said.

"I'm done," Thaddeus said, wiping his mouth and pushing away from the bar. "I suggest you watch your step."

"Don't say a word, promise me," Bart said.

"I won't say a thing, but Calvin might," Thaddeus said, acknowledging the fact Calvin had left upset.

"He won't say anything. I've known him too long; he'd never betray me," Bart said. "I think you should work with me on this. That's a lot of money."

Thaddeus grinned and replied, "My life is worth more." He turned and walked away.

Bart mumbled something under his breath and waved for the bartender to come over.

Seeing a unique opportunity and after being teased by Abigail showing him the wanted poster, Billy leaned over in Bart's direction and asked, "You looking for help?"

Bart leaned away from Billy, gave him a once-over, and asked, "You listening to my conversation?"

"I heard just a little, and I'm—"

Before Billy could finish, Bart drew his Colt and pointed it at Billy. "Curiosity killed the cat, they say."

Billy raised his hands and said, "Listen, I didn't mean no harm."

"But I do if you think you're going to threaten my uncle," Abigail said, her Colt drawn and aimed at Bart's face.

Bart hadn't seen Abigail until he was looking down the length of her pistol's barrel. "Where did you come from, little lady?"

"I'm sly. Now lower your pistol and set it on the bar," Abigail said with an air of confidence.

A broad smile stretched across Billy's face. Here was a small-framed girl who just seconds ago was enjoying a root beer with childish fervor and now had transformed into a gunfighter.

"I don't believe you'll shoot me," Bart sneered. "You're just a child."

"Are you willing to take that chance, huh?" Abigail asked.

"Maybe I am," Bart countered.

"This Colt I'm holding has a lighter trigger pull than most. All it takes is just a gentle squeeze and she'll fire.

Please don't make me show you," Abigail snapped.

A wide grin appeared on Bart's face, exposing his darkly stained teeth. His grin soon turned into a hearty laugh. He lowered his pistol but instead of setting it on the bar as ordered, he defied her and placed it back in his holster.

Abigail uncocked her pistol and did the same, but stood her ground near Bart, ensuring he didn't draw again.

"Now that we've sort of introduced ourselves, let me be a bit more formal. My name is Billy, and this is my niece, Abigail. I did hear you talking with your associates about the bounty, not because I was eavesdropping but because how could I not hear. You were talking so loud about it that I'm sure I'm not the only one who heard you talking."

Bart looked around and saw all eyes were on them. He swiveled and saw the bartender standing at a safe distance, wiping off a glass.

"How about we go find a table in the corner and talk?" Billy said.

Bart nodded.

As the three headed for a table, Abigail tugged on Billy's shirt and whispered, "What are you doing? I thought you didn't want to do this."

"I don't, consider this a lesson. I'll explain later," Billy said.

They all sat down.

"I won't waste your time, so I'll get right to the point. I'm a bounty hunter, and Abigail here is my…partner," Billy said.

Hearing her title as partner made Abigail perk up.

"You know for sure who killed this Indian woman and where to find him?" Billy asked.

"Yep, I sure do," Bart replied.

"Who is it?" Billy asked.

Goose bumps spread across Abigail's skin. This was so exciting for her.

"I'm not telling you anything. How do I know you just won't go and do the job for yourself? Nope, I won't say a word until I have some assurances."

"What can I say to make you feel better?" Billy asked.

"Who are you really?" Bart asked.

"I told you."

"And this girl is your partner? An old man and a young girl, I'm finding this hard to believe," Bart sneered.

"Do you want help or not?" Billy asked.

"You're serious? You want to collect the bounty?" Bart replied with a question, appearing stunned when he realized Billy might be serious.

"We are," Billy said, now feeling a bit uncomfortable. How far was he willing to take this ruse?

Bart thought for a second and said, "Meet me at the old livery later tonight, say midnight. We'll discuss the details."

"Very well," Billy said. He turned to Abigail and asked, "You ready to go, partner?"

Abigail nodded, squinting her eyes and furrowing her brow to appear determined and fearless.

The two rose and exited the bar. Outside, Abigail nudged Billy with her elbow and asked, "How are we going to sneak out later without Aunt Nell knowing?"

"We're not sneaking out. What you experienced was all you're going to. If we take it to the next level, things can get real dangerous. I wanted to give you a taste, nothing more."

"No, please, let's go meet him, see what we can find out," Abigail pleaded.

"We found out a lot even without meeting him. I know the man works for the Big Circle Ranch, that he's the son of the owner, that the owner is attempting to keep it quiet, and that the killer is at the ranch, somewhere. If Tillis and I were working this, we'd bypass the meeting, head directly for the ranch, and reconnoiter; that can take days. Once we felt comfortable that we had the lay of the land and where the killer might be, we'd make our move in the early morning hours under cover of night."

"Sounds so thrilling. How about we go reconnoiter?" Abigail urged.

"No, that's it; in fact, I exposed you too much. If your Aunt Nell found out, she'd have a bounty put on my head," Billy joked.

FORT COLLINS, COLORADO

August slowly dismounted his horse. His buttocks, back and legs were sore and tender after the ride from Denver. It had been eleven years since he'd ridden a horse, and his body was painfully telling him that. Grunting the entire way, he walked his horse to the closest livery and dropped him off. After buying the horse, he was left with very little, enough to buy food for a couple of weeks or a wild night in town, which for him was tempting. Brushing aside reason, he sauntered to the local bar and brothel and checked in.

"That'll be fifteen dollars for a girl and a room," Mack, the proprietor of the brothel, told him from behind the bar.

"Girls are only ten dollars in Denver," August protested loudly.

The people near him in the packed bar gave him a glance and quickly went back to drinking.

"Then go back to Denver," Mack quipped, turning his attention to a paying customer ordering a whiskey.

Fuming, August looked into the leather pouch, which held what remained of his inheritance, and grumbled, "Damn it." He knew he needed to be frugal, but his carnal desires were playing havoc with his reason. Being in an orphanage run by priests and nuns was not unlike being in a prison of sorts. Feeling he'd missed out on so many things, August was attempting in a matter of days to get his fill of those things he had been deprived of for eleven years. Holding several coins in his hand, he slammed them on the bar and said, "Fine, but I don't want an old fat woman, I want a young girl."

Mack returned upon hearing August consent to the price. "We don't have old fat women working here, and you need to define young girls, because we hold to a bit of morality here. No girls under eighteen."

"Eighteen, nineteen, that's fine," August said.

"I'll get you set up. Have a whiskey on me 'til then," Mack said, waving one of his men over. "Set him up with Marcie in room ten." The man nodded and headed upstairs. Mack turned and poured a glass of whiskey and slid it over to August. "What brings you to Fort Collins?"

"Passing through is all," August replied, taking the glass and tossing it back.

Mack poured him another and asked, "Heading where?"

"Montana," August answered.

"You wouldn't happen to be a bounty hunter, would you?"

Curious, August asked, "Why do you ask that?"

"Word has spread far and wide of a huge bounty to be had up in Miles City, Montana."

"What's huge?" August asked, taking the glass and holding it firmly in his grasp.

"Seven thousand, but rumors say the man who put the bounty out may hike it even higher."

"Seven thousand is a lot of money. Who's the bounty on?" August asked, genuinely curious.

"That's the thing, poster doesn't have a name. Those seeking to secure it must find out who the killers are then bring them in, dead or alive, and they must show proof they were the killers," Mack explained.

"Who did they kill, a queen or something?" August asked.

"Get this, some Indian woman. Yep, one of the

largest bounties around, and it's for the killers of an Indian woman." Mack laughed.

"What's so funny about that?" August asked, not seeing the humor.

Mack leaned in and furrowed his brow in confusion. "She's a brown-skinned savage, she's half human, and she's getting a bounty that's set aside for royalty."

"She was someone's wife and daughter, maybe even someone's mother, and you find it humorous that someone would care enough to post a bounty?"

Mack pulled away the whiskey bottle and said, "Room ten, Marcie is waiting on you."

Seeing he'd worn out his welcome with Mack, August finished his whiskey and headed up to meet his entertainment for the night.

CHAPTER FOUR

ROCKLAND, IDAHO TERRITORY

AUGUST 24, 1888

Grant woke to a coughing fit worse than he'd ever experienced. He sprang from the bed and to the basin on the chest of drawers. There he stood, hacking and coughing until he spit up a large amount of blood. Standing above the basin, blood dripping from his lips, he pondered how long he really had. Was it a month? Maybe two? Could he last long enough to ensure paying off the past-due fee to the territorial government and still have enough in reserve for George and Margaret to survive off of if they had a bad crop? Maybe they should sell the farm, pay the fee, and head to California, have them get established, but doing what? Would he even survive the trek? So many questions plagued and tortured his mind but didn't alleviate his concerns for them. If it were just him, he'd go out for a last ride, tear it up a bit, and go out the way he came in, kicking and screaming. The thing was, he did have them to look after; he'd made that promise to his wife just before she died. He could fantasize about riding off into the sunset, but it wasn't going to happen. He needed a plan, he needed something that could give him access to a large sum of money and quickly. Could he go out and try to collect a bounty? He could, but most were small. No, he needed one that was large enough, he needed the perfect job—one quick and relatively easy job that paid a hell of a lot—but where would he find that? It just seemed like fantasy again, so he dashed those thoughts and brought his mind to ponder how he'd handle the debt and his legacy to his children in a way that was reasonable.

A tap at the door tore him away from his beleaguered thoughts.

"Yes," he called out.

"Pa, you okay?" Margaret asked.

The glow from a lantern shone under the door and illuminated the floor.

"It's open," Grant said.

Margaret opened the door but stood at the doorway. "Do you need anything?"

Grant wiped the blood from his lips and chin and replied, "Woke up coughing badly. I'll be fine."

She stepped farther into the room but paused from going to the basin for fear she'd see blood. "Can I get you anything, a glass of water maybe?"

"That would be great, thank you," he said.

She rushed from the room and returned promptly with a tin cup filled with cool water. She handed it to him and said, "Here ya go. Can I cook you anything?"

"It's early still, I think. The water is enough," he said before gulping down the cup. The water was refreshing and soothed his sore throat.

"Pa?"

"Yes, sweetheart," he said.

"I'm scared."

He put the cup down and went to her. He wrapped his arms around her and squeezed. "It'll all be fine in the end. Death is a part of life, and for some reason God's decided my time is coming sooner rather than later. I look at it this way, he knows you and your brother are mature enough to handle yourselves now. Consider that a compliment from him."

"A compliment? I hate him," she scowled.

"Now, now, we don't say that. Come sit down," he said, escorting her to his bedside. The two sat down on the edge of the bed. "God never said believing in him would ensure your life didn't have struggle. He never guaranteed that you'd be without pain or suffering. All he guaranteed you was that during those times, he would be there with you."

"If he's here with me, then he should stop this and heal you. I want him to give us a miracle," Margaret said sadly.

Grant chuckled and said, "Me too."

"What are we going to do about the farm?" Margaret asked.

"I was just thinking about that. I don't have the answer, but I'll figure it out. What I encourage you and your brother to do is think hard about it as well. I'm open to all suggestions. Doesn't mean I'll use them, but I want you two to think for yourselves, be creative, innovative."

"I can do that," she said.

"Good, now back to bed," he said, kissing her forehead.

She hopped up and left the room, closing the door

behind her.

Grant sat, his mind racing back to the many questions from before. Suddenly a new question popped into his mind. Was this some sort of punishment from God? He had committed many sins in his early life, with a few standing out that could only be described as barbaric. Was he now being punished for those crimes? Had his past finally come back to haunt him? Would the ghosts of his youth be revisited upon him and his family? He had hoped that his change in lifestyle and confession of guilt to God in his prayers had been enough, but maybe it wasn't. Maybe a man was to suffer the real consequences of his actions in his life on Earth, not just in the afterlife. He thought he'd been lucky, as nothing had happened to him, but maybe one was meant to pay the debt of the sins they'd committed. If that were the case, the payment for his past was a steep price.

ROSEBUD, MONTANA TERRITORY

The crashing of the front door being kicked in woke Abigail. She sat up, confused and scared, as she heard men in the front room hollering and screaming. Instinctually, she leapt from her bed, grabbed her gun belt first, then made for the bedroom door. She opened it to find Nell coming her way, waving her arms erratically.

"Back inside your room, hurry!" Nell hollered.

The hall and room beyond Nell were lit with the glow of torches.

Abigail stepped back into her room, with Nell

coming in right behind her. Nell slammed the door shut and pushed a small dresser in front of it.

"What's going on?" Abigail asked.

"Men barged in. They have your uncle Billy, and they're asking for you too," she said, her voice cracking with fear.

Abigail instantly suspected what might be happening.

"I had gone to the outhouse when I heard the noise. I ran in through the back door and to you as fast as I could."

Heavy footfalls followed by the jingling of the knob told them the men were just on the other side of the door. "Come on out, Abigail!" Jed hollered.

"Out the window, go, now!" Nell ordered. She raced to the window, opened it up and barked, "Go, run as fast and far as your legs will take you."

"I won't leave you or Uncle Billy," Abigail declared, pulling out her pistol.

Nell lowered her hand that held the Colt and said, "There's too many, and now is not the time to fight. You'll only die too."

Loud banging boomed from the door.

"Go now!" Nell ordered.

"Come with me," Abigail pleaded.

"I'm going to distract them, give you time to flee. Now go!" Nell sternly commanded.

Abigail wanted to stay but was ever obedient. She climbed out the window, hit the ground, and sprinted away from the house.

Nell closed the window just as the door burst open.

In came Bart followed by two men. "Who are you?"

"Who the hell are you?" Nell snapped back defiantly.

"Where's the girl?" Jed asked.

"There's no girl here," Nell declared.

Frustrated, Bart stepped forward, took a handful of Nell's hair, and pushed her out the door and down the hall.

"Let go of me," Nell hollered.

Bart ignored her. He escorted her through the house and out front, where Billy was on his knees surrounded by six other men, all holding a weapon in one hand and a torch in the other. Sitting atop a horse was Boyd. Bart threw her to the ground next to Billy, who took her into his arms and cradled her. "You okay?"

"I'm fine, but I'm not okay with these scoundrels being here!" Nell spat.

"Where's the girl?" Bart asked, stepping in front of Billy.

"She's not here," Billy said.

"Then where is she?" Bart howled.

"You think I'd ever tell you anything, huh?" Billy asked.

Bart raised his arm high above his head and was about to come down hard against Billy's head when Boyd cried out, "That's enough!"

Bart froze and turned to Boyd. "I'll beat the information out of them."

"Step aside," Boyd ordered.

"Who are you, and why are you terrorizing me and my husband?" Nell shouted.

"Ma'am, I'm here solely because your husband and his niece met my man Bart today in a bar in Miles City and claimed they were going after my son with hopes to collect a bounty."

"That's a lie!" Nell snapped.

"I can assure you it isn't. Ask your husband," Boyd said calmly.

Nell turned her head towards Billy and said, "This is all a lie; tell me it is."

"I wasn't serious. I was merely showing Abigail how we used to do it years ago. It was supposed to be a lesson, nothing more."

"A lesson? William Roscoe…what have you done?" Nell screamed.

"It was meant to be a lesson, nothing more," Billy pleaded to Boyd.

"A lesson? You expect me to believe that?" Boyd said, shifting in his saddle. He cleared his throat and said, "I own this town, I have ears everywhere, and I make it my business to know who lives here." Boyd paused for a second then continued. "You're William Roscoe Bartlett, you are a bounty hunter and used to ride with the notorious Hammer Tillis. I know who you are, but I thought you'd given up that life. Then earlier today you start talking to Bart about collecting that bounty, and in order to do so, you probably were going to invade my ranch and try to snatch my boy, who, by the way, has been wrongfully accused of that poor woman's murder."

"Boyd, I wasn't being serious. My niece has expressed a desire to be a bounty hunter, and it's something I encourage but only for her to fantasize over, nothing more. I heard Bart here talking about the bounty, so I thought it would be fun to show off for the niece."

Nell slapped Billy hard and yelled, "Fun? You think this is fun?"

"I have men planted in town to ferret out snakes like you. I can't be having people in town causing trouble and interfering with business, all for a small bounty," Boyd said. Bart stepped out from the group of men behind Boyd. "You see him; this is Bart. I had him go into town and start sniffing out bounty hunters."

"It will never happen again," Billy declared.

"You're right it won't," Boyd said. He whistled and waved Jed over. "Son, you started this. Finish it."

Jed walked up to Billy, aimed his pistol, and shot Billy in the face.

Billy fell backwards dead.

Nell let out a wail in grief and grabbed Billy's dead body. "No! What have you done?"

"Where's the girl?" Boyd asked.

Nell faced Boyd and stood up. "I'll never tell you, never!"

"Then you don't care if you die?" Boyd asked.

"Kill me. You'll never get her," Nell declared.

Abigail had run until she spotted a large boulder about two hundred yards away. She hid behind it and caught her breath. Her entire body was shaking, and her mind raced with what would happen next. Upon hearing the gunshot, she peered over the boulder and saw Billy fall to the ground. Her heart sank. She wanted to run back and shoot them all, but Nell was right, there were too many and she'd only die too. Frozen in fear, she watched like a voyeur as Nell was shot like Billy.

Nell fell to the ground next to Billy, their hands touching.

Jed holstered his pistol and asked, "Now what, Father?"

"Put their bodies in the house and burn it," Boyd ordered.

Men immediately started doing as he said.

"And the girl?" Jed asked.

"She'll show up soon enough, but let this be a message that anyone who wishes to hurt my family will be met with the full force of my power."

Clement appeared and asked, "Should I send out men in all directions looking for her?"

"No, her word will mean nothing, but if someone does find her, you know what to do," Boyd said, pulling on the reins of his horse and riding off into the black of the night.

Tears flowed freely from Abigail. All her mind kept repeating was that this had been her fault. She had pressured Billy about the bounty, and all he had been doing was giving her a taste of what she wanted. He had been right that this was a dangerous world, bad men did exist, evil men did walk the same earth as her, and they were deliberate men, they didn't hesitate to kill. Her grief turned to anger. She wiped the tears from her face and made a declaration that she'd avenge her aunt and uncle, but she knew she couldn't do it alone. She needed help, and she knew where she might be able to find it.

CHAPTER FIVE

ROCKLAND, IDAHO TERRITORY

AUGUST 27, 1888

The smell of bacon and fried eggs cooking lured Grant from his bedroom. Like the day before, he had slept in longer than normal mainly because his coughing kept him up. When he emerged from his bedroom, he found George sitting at the dining table in the kitchen and Margaret at the stove.

"Good morning," he said, scratching his head. On his face sat a week's worth of thick stubble. He normally kept his face clean shaven, but since the coughing and heavy fatigue, he'd given up and decided to save what little energy he had for working around the farm.

"Hi, Pa," George said, not looking up from his plate as he shoveled a forkful of eggs into his mouth.

Margaret stepped away from the stove, came over, and gave him a kiss on the cheek. "Good morning, Pa. How are you feeling this morning?"

"Good, I'm ready to start work on those bushels today," he said, taking a seat at the head of the table.

Margaret promptly served up two eggs over easy and two pieces of fatty bacon.

Grant stared at the food in front of him. He loved bacon and eggs, but his stomach was telling him something different that morning, but he wouldn't let

Margaret's hard work go to waste, so he carved up the eggs and began to eat.

Margaret filled a plate for herself and sat next to him. She watched him eat, looking for any new signs that his sickness had gotten worse.

Noticing her stares, he lifted his head and said, "Nothing's changed."

"I'm just concerned, forgive me," she said, feeling embarrassed.

"If Pa says he's fine, he's fine," George said.

"I believe him. I'm…oh, enough," she snapped, shoving her plate away from her.

"Don't be grumpy," George growled.

"I'm not grumpy, I'm sad!" she fired back at George.

"Enough, you two," Grant barked.

They looked at him, both stewing and itching for a fight with the other.

"I'm not going to let this disease tear apart our family. No matter how angry or sad you might be, we're a family, and after I'm gone, you two are going to need each other."

"Sorry, Margaret," George said.

"I'm sorry too," she replied.

Wanting to shift the topic, he said, "How come I don't see you both studying your French language book?"

"I don't have time; plus, what good will French do me on a potato farm?" George said just as he bit a piece of bacon.

"And what's your excuse?" Grant asked Margaret.

"Similar to George's," she answered.

"Your mother wanted you two to be fluent in her native tongue. I think you should continue," Grant said.

"But no one speaks French around here. This is America; we all speak English," George said.

"Not true, go to Texas or the Southwest and many people speak Spanish. Heck, around here you can go just east and you might run into a Crow."

"Pa, you're being silly," George said.

"I'm not being silly. In all my travels there were more than a few times I wished I could speak or understand other languages. Listen, you two, learning another language doesn't mean you'll know English less, it only means you'll know another way to speak. It expands your base of knowledge."

"If it doesn't grow or sell potatoes for me, I don't see the point," George countered.

"Then do it for your mother's memory," Grant said. "Can you do that?"

They both nodded.

"Margaret, do you remember that Mama used to pronounce your name Mar-gar-eeet when you were a baby? I don't know when we stopped, but before long we started just calling you Mar-gar-et."

"Was her accent beautiful?" Margaret asked.

"It was lovely, it was the first thing that drew me to her, and her eyes, it felt like she was seeing into me. It was almost scary, but assuring too; it's hard to explain," Grant said, his mind racing back and reliving the first time he and Latanne had met.

"I remember her accent," George said.

"I do too, but sometimes I wonder if it's just a dream," Margaret said.

"I'll tell you what, tonight, let's all study French together. How does that sound?" Grant asked.

"Wonderful," Margaret replied.

"I'd like that," George answered.

"Good, that sounds like a plan. Now, let's finish up here and start our day," Grant said.

MILES CITY, MONTANA TERRITORY

Going into town was Colton's least favorite thing to do, but today's journey was as important as the day he'd ordered the wanted posters made.

He made his way down the muddy streets to the law office of Frederick Busey. Today he needed to create an insurance policy, so to speak. After hearing about Billy and Nell, he suspected something awful or nefarious had occurred and speculated that it had something to do with Martha, the wanted poster, and the Big Circle Ranch. Of course, he didn't have any evidence of it, but something felt wrong.

He tied up his horse and entered the small, eight-by-eight-foot-square office space to find Frederick relaxing in his desk chair with his legs kicked up. "Mr. Busey, I need your legal assistance."

"Mr. Emery, how do you do?" Frederick said, sitting up and removing his feet from his desk.

Pulling up a spare chair, Colton took a seat. "You've worked for me over the years, specifically with contracts, and I've come to find you to be honest, trustworthy, professional and discreet."

"Why, thank you for the kind words. What can I do for you today?" Frederick asked.

"You no doubt have heard about Martha's murder and about the subsequent wanted posters I've had made and circulated?"

"Yes, I have, and let me give you my condolences on the death of your wife," Frederick said somberly.

"Frederick, I need you to open an escrow account for me," Colton said.

"For what?"

"The bounty money, I need to ensure that money is out of my hands and in an escrow account, protected by the law and insured."

"That's unorthodox."

"It may be, but it's necessary. I also need you to draft a will for me and instructions as to the payout of the bounty. Oh, and I need you to draft a power of attorney; it will be for you to act on my behalf in the event I die."

"Die?"

"Will you do this for me?" Colton asked, almost sounding desperate.

"Yes, of course."

"Good," Colton said, opening a leather case and placing it on the table. "Inside you'll find ten thousand dollars. That's the bounty money plus an extra three thousand; I'll explain what that's for in a bit."

Frederick slid the case close to him and peered in. Inside, the bag was a quarter of the way filled with stacked bills. "You are serious."

"I don't believe in wasting people's time. Please can you do what I've asked?"

"I already said I would. What would you like to work on first?" Frederick asked.

"The instructions for the bounty first, then my will," Colton replied.

Frederick took a pen, dipped it into an inkwell, and began to write. He paused, looked at Colton, and asked, "Please be specific and detail just how you want the bounty handled."

WEST OF BILLINGS, MONTANA TERRITORY

If Abigail was one thing, it was quick thinking. After witnessing the brutal murders of Uncle Billy and Aunt Nell, she patiently waited until Boyd's men retreated and the house fire died out. When it was safe, she went back to the house, got a horse, took some old clothes from a steamer trunk in the barn, and dug up a Mason jar full of gold coins that Billy had mentioned was buried near a small tree in the back. If she was going to head west to Idaho, she'd need money for her trip.

After passing through Billings, she made camp on the banks of the Yellowstone River. There she planned on spending her eighteenth birthday honing her skills.

Uncle Billy had taught her many things over the years: riding a horse, shooting, throwing tomahawks, and how to fight with a knife. However, she also took the crafts and homesteading skills that Nell had taught her to heart as well. She knew how to hunt an elk, kill it, dress it, prepare the meat for a meal, and tan the hide—all skills for which she had her aunt and uncle to thank.

Uncle Billy always told her to be as well-rounded skill wise as possible because you never knew when you might need it, and now she needed it, and she could never have known it was going to happen. Not only were they both caring and nurturing, they were wise.

As she sat along the river and watched it flow past, she began to run scenarios on how she'd present her case to Grant, with hopes she could enlist him in her cause. Having never met him, she could only guess how their interaction would go.

A scream in the distance tore her away from her thoughts. She looked around but couldn't pinpoint where it came from. A second scream echoed down the river channel; this time she was able to locate where it was coming from. She hopped to her feet and ran towards where she'd heard it. What concerned her the most was the scream definitely was coming from a child. Clearing a small rise, she spotted a small house with several outbuildings. No one could be seen outside, but there was evidence of someone living there, from the clothes drying on a line.

Unsure of what she could be walking into, she paused her advance and took cover behind a tree.

A third scream wailed from the house, followed by a young girl bursting through the front door and running towards her.

Emerging from the open doorway was a man; in his

hands he held a belt. His face was flush and his eyes wide with anger. "You come back here!" he bellowed.

That phrase sent shivers down Abigail's spine. It was similar to what her father would say after she fled his abuse.

The girl didn't heed his words, and she kept running towards the tree where Abigail was taking cover.

"You think that was bad, I'll beat you worse when you come home, and believe me, you'll be coming home soon enough," the man hollered, slamming the door behind him.

The girl cleared the rise and jumped behind the tree where Abigail was hiding. Upon seeing her, she cried out in surprise that anyone would be there. "Don't hurt me."

Abigail held up her finger to her mouth and said softly, "I won't hurt you."

The girl wasn't so sure and scooted far enough away to be out of Abigail's reach.

Seeing the fear and apprehension, Abigail sat back and asked, "What did you do?"

"Nothin'," she answered.

"My father used to beat me for no reason too," Abigail said.

"That man isn't my father," the girl said.

"Who is he?" Abigail asked.

"Who are you?" the girl asked.

"Abigail, but my friends call me Abby. You can call me that if you'd like."

"What are you doing here?"

"I'm camping just down there along the river and

heard screaming. I came up to see what was going on and if I can help," Abigail explained.

"You can kill that son of a bitch," the girl spat out.

Abigail raised her brows in shock at the girl's foul mouth. She must have been ten or so, but had the anger of an adult pent up inside her.

"If you can't do that, leave me alone," she said.

"You know my name. What's yours?" Abigail asked.

"Madeleine…"

"And let me guess, your friends call you Maddy?" Abigail asked, hoping to bring levity to the conversation.

"I don't have any friends," Madeleine said sadly.

"I'll be your friend," Abigail said.

Madeleine buried her head in her hands and started to cry.

"I know what you're going through," Abigail said, scooting closer.

"And what did you do?" Madeleine asked, her voice muffled.

Abigail took a second to think about how to answer and decided to be brutally honest. "I killed him."

Madeleine's head popped up. "You did?"

"Yeah," Abigail said, feeling a tinge of pride saying it.

"How? Did you shoot him?" Madeleine asked, looking at Abigail's Colt that sat snuggling in her holster.

Abigail nodded and said, "Yep."

"I want to kill my stepfather. He hurts me," Madeleine said.

"Is your mother not around?"

"She's there, but she's scared to upset him, so she

takes his side."

Rustling behind Abigail startled her. She turned and was face-to-face with the muzzle of a shotgun. "What are you doing?" a woman barked.

Abigail raised her hands and replied, "Just talking, nothing more."

"Madeleine, get up and come home. Your father isn't done with you yet," Madeleine's mother snapped, her eyes bulging and veins popping on her neck.

"Mama, please, let me stay outside for a while," Madeleine pleaded.

"Get your butt inside now or it will be worse," Madeleine's mother barked.

Abigail shifted slightly.

"You move, I'll put buckshot in ya, you hear me?"

"Why are you letting your husband beat your daughter? What sort of mother are you?" Abigail asked, her anger rising.

"You mind your own damn business and get off our land, you hear?"

"I was just talking to Madeleine, providing her some much-needed comfort," Abigail said.

"Madeleine, you get up now or I swear, girl, that beatin' will be so bad you won't sit for a week," Madeleine's mother snarled.

"Please, Mama, please," Madeleine cried.

"What's going on out there?" the father hollered as he emerged from the house. He pulled up his suspenders, and in his hands he held an axe. "Sophie, who you talkin' to out there?"

Sophie growled at Abigail, "You best be gettin'. If he comes out here, you're gonna regret it too."

Abigail slowly and carefully got to her feet, ensuring that she never turned her back towards Sophie. "I'm leavin'."

Madeleine gave one last look towards Abigail and mouthed the words, "HELP ME."

Faced with a shotgun leveled at her and a deranged stepfather coming her way with an axe, Abigail felt like any attempt would end in failure. She had gotten fast at drawing, but she couldn't beat a person who had a gun leveled at her, and trying would be suicide. With this realization, she backed away. "Goodbye, Madeleine."

With Abigail a good thirty feet away, Sophie grabbed Madeleine firmly and shook her. "Damn it, girl. You're always causing me and everyone else trouble. Get home now," Sophie growled as she shoved Madeleine.

Madeleine wailed in pain and cried for mercy from her mother and stepfather, who was now there delivering on the abuse he'd promised her.

Memories of her own abuse suddenly surfaced and triggered anxiety in Abigail. She turned and sprinted to her campsite. When she arrived, she hastily packed her things, loaded up her horse, and rode away as fast as she could.

ROCK SPRINGS, WYOMING

August had made it out of Colorado, but his drinking and outright debauchery had put the brakes on going farther past the small mining town of Rock Springs, Wyoming. Out of money, and now without a horse, having sold it the day before to pay for his pleasures, he found himself begging for food on the street.

Rock Springs was a town filled with hardworking people. Many of the men worked in the mines while their wives ensured the households were kept up; with so many risking their lives to put food on the table, seeing someone loiter and beg on their streets didn't sit well.

After a full day holding out his hand and with not a penny to show for it, August grew increasingly resentful of the townspeople, and more nefarious means of getting money began to come to mind, until a middle-aged and beautiful woman by the name of Liza approached him.

"Are you hungry?" she asked, holding a sack of provisions, mainly canned food she'd just purchased from the mercantile.

"I am. Any amount you can spare will be helpful," he pleaded, holding out his filthy hand.

She gave him a pleasant smile and said, "I can't offer you money, but I can make you a hot meal."

He grumbled at the offer because he mainly wanted to drink.

"I'm making beans, peas and I have a ham at home," she said.

He glanced at her necklace and saw several stones glisten in the fading light of the sun. Changing his tune, he asked, "Are you inviting me to your house for a meal?"

"I am," she said sweetly.

On her left hand he spotted a gold band signaling

she was married, which prompted him to ask, "How will your husband feel about you taking in a bum?"

"He wouldn't mind," she replied.

"Then I accept your most generous offer," he said, getting to his feet and slapping off the dirt and dust from his trousers.

"Then come with me. My house is just at the end of the street," she said.

He picked up what he had left, which included his rifle and saddlebags, and walked beside her down the street.

As they passed a few people, they gave him hard stares while exchanging looks of disapproval with her.

"Don't pay no attention to them. The one problem about being in such a small town is it comes with small minds," she quipped.

He laughed.

"What's your name?" she asked.

"Augustus, but everyone calls me August," he answered.

"My name is Liza, that's short for Elizabeth. I've been in Rock Springs for a little over three years. And you, where are you from?"

"Denver," he said.

"I've never been. I hear it's fast becoming a great place to call home," she said, her eyes widening with joy at the prospect of moving.

The two continued on until they reached her front door. She went to turn the knob, but before she could, the door opened wide. "Hi, Ma," a young boy, about eleven, said.

"Michael, have you cleaned up yet? Dinner will be on the table in twenty minutes," Liza said, walking inside followed by August.

Michael gave August a wary glance.

"This is August. He's going to join us for dinner," Liza said. "In fact, why don't you take him with you so he can get cleaned up too."

Michael nodded and walked off, with August following him. Michael took him out back. There he pointed to a small table, a deep metal basin, and a hand pump. "Soap is on the side."

"Thanks," August said as he pumped water into the basin. "Say, where's your father?"

Michael raised a single brow and replied, "My pa is dead, died in the mine shaft collapse a year ago."

"Dead?"

"Why are you here?" Michael asked.

Toweling off, August answered, "I was in need, and your mother is providing, as simple as that." He looked around the back and spotted a small henhouse and a little shed. "You have a horse in there?"

Michael shook his head and said, "We have one old horse, my father's. What is it you need?" Michael asked, cluing in that August wasn't to be trusted.

August tossed the towel at Michael and said, "Food, nothing more." Leaving Michael at the basin, he went back inside to find Liza in the kitchen preparing the meal.

"I have some chilled tea. Would you care for some?" she asked.

"Sounds great," August answered.

Liza poured him a glass and set it on the table. "Please, sit."

August took the glass and took a sip. It was good, but what would taste great for him right about now was a tall glass of whiskey instead.

"I make it the day before, then place it in the bottle, and lower it into the well. The water keeps it cool."

"It's good."

"Tell me, August, how is it you're down on your luck?" Liza asked, carving slices off the ham.

"Just bad luck," he lied.

"Too much drink, maybe?" Liza asked, giving him a look to see his response.

"Nope, no drinking," he again lied.

She stepped away from the ham and walked up to him. "I can see it. My husband had a taste for it too. It would change is personality. After his death, I rediscovered the Lord, and in Him, I've gotten salvation. He teaches us that we should care for those in need, and when I saw you, I knew I had to help."

"It's much appreciated," he said, taking a large gulp of tea.

"All I ask is that you respect my house and my rules."

"Of course," he said.

"Good, then please remove your gun belt and leave it at the front door. You can hang it on the wall, there's a couple of pegs."

He chuckled and stood up. "Sure thing."

Michael came into the kitchen just as August was leaving to hang up his gun belt. He marched over to Liza and whispered, "I don't trust him."

"Now, Michael, what have I told you? God puts people in need in our way to test us, to see if we're living up to his word."

"But—"

"No buts, we have a guest for dinner. Now go set the table; I'll be serving in a few minutes," Liza ordered firmly.

Michael did as he was told, only protesting through his demeanor.

August returned to find Michael scowling and giving him what could only be described as a *stink eye*. "Can I help?"

"No," Michael replied.

"Okay, boys, please sit down," Liza said, coming to the table with a large platter graced with ham, beans and peas.

"I'm not a boy; I'm eighteen," August countered, not liking being referenced to as a child.

"Then I apologize, young man," she said, smiling. "Michael is still a boy, though, being he's only eleven."

***

The three ate dinner, with Liza asking many questions of August and him giving answers as vague as he could. The single kerosene lantern lit the room just enough, tossing their shadows on the far wall.

Though dim, the light kept casting off her necklace, making him continuously stare at it through the dinner. He wondered how much he could sell it for along with the silver candelabras he'd seen that graced the mantel in the living room. It wouldn't take much to steal them, just brandish his gun, tell her to remove them, grab the candelabras, tie them up, get the horse, and ride off. He'd be several towns northwest by the time they got free or were found.

"Ma, can I have a piece of pie?" Michael asked.

"Of course, we shall all have a piece," she said, picking up the plates and heading towards the counter behind her.

August looked around for anything else of value but saw nothing. However, she must have cash or coin somewhere, he thought.

"Do you want a piece of apple pie?" she asked August, who was lost in thought. "Hello, August?"

He blinked heavily and said, "Um, yes, sure."

"Good, I'll go get it," she said, going and pulling a pie dish from a shelf.

Anxious to get moving, he stood up and said, "If you'll excuse me, but nature calls."

"Out back to the left," she said, slicing the pie.

"Great," he said, exiting the kitchen. He walked down a short hall until he arrived at the front door. There, on the wall to his right, was his gun belt hanging where he'd hung it up. He took it off the wall and immediately noticed it weighed less. He looked quickly and saw his pistol was missing.

"You looking for this?" Michael asked.

August spun around.

From the shadows, Michael stepped out holding August's pistol. "Are you here to rob us?"

"Listen, boy, put that down," August said, his left hand out in front of him in a protective manner.

"My pa taught me how to shoot. You pull this back," Michael said, using both thumbs to cock the hammer. "And when that's done, you put your finger—"

Not waiting to find out if Michael could shoot him, August reached for the barrel of his Colt, took it firmly in his hand, and yanked it out of Michael's grasp. He flipped it around and pointed it at Michael. "Boy, turn around if you know what's good for ya."

"Ma?" Michael cried out.

Shaking his head in frustration, August swung the pistol high and slammed the butt of the grip against the top of Michael's head.

Michael grunted then dropped to the floor with a thud, unconscious.

Liza heard Michael call her name and the commotion and appeared in the hallway. "Michael?" she asked. When she saw him on the floor and August towering over him holding a pistol, she gasped. "Oh, dear Lord."

"Liza, hand it over," August snapped, his hand trembling with nervous energy.

"What have you done? He's a boy," she asked, bending down and cradling Michael's limp, lifeless body into her arms.

"He's alive, just out cold. Now hand it over," he

demanded, pointing at her neck.

"You want this?" she asked, confused.

"Yes, hand it over," he barked.

"It's not worth anything. It's costume jewelry, nothing more," she said, caressing Michael's face.

"Don't lie!" he snapped, bending down and yanking it off her neck with a hard pull. He examined it quickly then stuffed it in his front pocket. "Now where's the cash, your coins?"

"I don't have much, only twenty-two dollars, but I need that for food," she moaned. "I let you into my home, I fed you. I showed you sympathy and compassion, and this is how you repay me?"

A nauseous feeling began to well up inside him as doubt filled him. Had he done the right thing? "Where's the money?"

"My bedroom, on the dresser, there's a small tin box," she answered.

With the pistol still cocked, he leveled it at her head and growled, "You'd better not be yelling, you hear me!"

"I'm not. Go get the money and get out of my house!" she wailed, tears of fear streaming down her face as she rocked back and forth with Michael in her arms.

Sweat clung to August's brow, and his heart was beating fast. He raced to the bedroom but couldn't see anything. Feeling around in the dark, he found the dresser and soon found the tin box. He took it and exited the bedroom. Back in the hallway, where he could see, he opened it up and saw a handful of coins nestled among trinkets.

"Take the coins and go," she spat.

He took the coins, dumped them in his pocket, and dropped the box on the hardwood floor. He spun around, grabbed the candelabras, and tucked them under his right arm. Feeling she wouldn't try anything, he uncocked his Colt and shoved it in his waistband.

"Leave!" she yelled.

"Shut your mouth, no yelling or I'll...I'll!" he hollered.

"You're going to hit me too?"

"Shut up!" he barked.

"You're a coward. You're not a man, you're a boy."

Angry, he marched over to her and yelled, "Shut up."

"What are you going to do...boy...hit a woman now?" she lambasted.

Unable to control his anger, he recoiled and struck her hard on the side of the face.

The strike was so hard, her head bounced off the wall, with her temple taking the greatest blow. She cried out then passed out.

He stared down at her limp body and saw a trickle of blood come from the side of her head. Fear filled him. Had he killed her? Not wanting to stay around to find out, he grabbed the rest of his personal items and fled out the back door. He sprinted to the small barn, flung open the door, and looked around, but he couldn't see a thing. He set everything on the ground and reached out to feel for a lantern. After a short search he found one sitting on a windowsill; next to it were matches. He lit the match then lit the lantern. When the warm orange glow illuminated the space, he looked around and saw the horse nervously standing in a stall, staring at him. Not wanting to waste any more time, he saddled the horse, attached his saddlebags, and loaded his stolen wares.

"Help!" a faint voice cried out from the house.

August listened.

"Help!" The voice grew louder.

It was Michael, and it sounded as if he was outside calling for help.

Knowing his time was up, he mounted the horse and jabbed the heels of his boots into the horse's ribs.

The horse reared for a second before sprinting out of the barn.

August pulled the reins hard to the left, turning the horse completely around, and once more jammed his heels into its sides.

The horse bolted away at top speed.

August didn't know what direction he was going; he only knew he needed to get out of there before someone answered Michael's call.

CHAPTER SIX

NORTH OF EAGLE ROCK, IDAHO TERRITORY

AUGUST 30, 1888

Abigail paced back and forth, looking at the map. With each mile she was drawing closer to Rockland. Her patience was running thin and so was life on the trail. She promised herself that the next town she'd stop at a hotel and get a proper bath, and according to the map, the next large town was Pocatello. Staying in a hotel would also distract her; the past few days all she kept hearing in her head was Madeleine's screaming and pleading. Regret had stayed with her since she had run off, unable and incapable of doing something to help her. She didn't regret taking the risk while under the threat of being shot; no, she regretted not going back immediately and freeing the poor girl.

A brisk wind came in from the north, blowing the hat off her head and jolting her to the present. She chased after the tumbling hat until she grabbed it. Frustrated, she held the hat tightly in her grip, bending the brim.

Madeleine's scream came back to her. She pressed her eyes closed and tried to force the images of the little girl out of her mind, but she couldn't. She was now haunted by her, and she knew the only thing that would eventually let her move on was to free her from the life of abuse she was living. She opened her eyes and looked up into the darkening clouds that were forming above her.

"Lord, watch over Madeleine, give her strength, and tell her in whatever way you can that soon she won't have to live the life she's living, that soon she'll be free. I say this prayer in your name, amen."

Several raindrops hit her face. Seconds later the sky opened up and a torrent of heavy rain began to fall from the sky.

Abigail stood unflinching as the rain pummeled her. She stretched out her arms and kept her face pointed to the sky.

"Hear me, Lord. Let me be your instrument on earth. Let me be a warrior for those who can't fight. Give me the power and wisdom that will be needed to protect the innocent and shield them from a life of torture, pain and suffering. I know this is what I was born for. Please, Lord, let me be your servant to help those in need," she prayed.

MILES CITY, MONTANA TERRITORY

Colton arrived in town, but this time, the angst he normally felt was gone. His visit with the attorney had cemented the bounty and ensured that no matter what, even in his absence, justice could be served.

With a feeling of contentment, he rode for the Elk's Head Saloon. He knew Boyd's men frequented the establishment, but today he'd enjoy a drink or two, and today he had an occasion—it was his and Marth's wedding anniversary.

When he arrived at the Elk's Head, he paused to think about his decision. Was he being foolish? he asked himself. Brushing aside his concerns, he pushed the swinging doors open and stepped into the smoke-filled room. From wall to wall, the place was filled with drunk ranch hands from the Big Circle Ranch. He gave them all a quick glance then strode in confidently and squeezed into a space at the bar.

He raised his right hand and said, "Bartender, whiskey."

Recognizing him immediately, the bartender walked up and leaned in close so he could whisper, "You shouldn't be in here."

"Am I not allowed here? Will you not serve me?" Colton asked.

"It's not that and you know it," the bartender warned.

"I'm here to have a couple of drinks to celebrate my wedding anniversary. Can't I do that without worrying about something happening to me?" he asked, knowing his question was meaningless.

Frustrated that Colton wouldn't listen, the bartender turned around, snatched a bottle from behind him, and slammed it down on the bar in front of Colton. He followed up with a shot glass. "Drink what you will, then leave; and if something goes south, don't look to me for help. You're on your own."

"I don't need your help. Didn't need it after I married my Martha and everyone ostracized me, and I don't need it now," Colton said. He took the bottle, pulled the cork with his teeth, and filled the glass full. He picked it up and swallowed it down with a single swig. He filled it again and repeated.

Seeing that he wasn't going to adhere to logic, the bartender walked away from Colton. "Damn fool."

Colton filled his glass a third time, but as he lifted it, a hand shot in and blocked its rise.

"Well, look who's in here having a drink? If it isn't the resident Indian lover," Jed said, slurring his words.

Colton cocked his head and asked, "Do you have to do that?"

"As a matter of fact, I do," Jed replied.

Ignoring him, Colton brought the glass out from underneath Jed's hand and tossed it back. "Do you mind? I'm here to celebrate something special."

Jed got into Colton's face and asked, "And what's that?"

Tuck, one of Boyd's loyal men, came from behind Jed and whispered, "Leave him alone."

Annoyed that he'd been reprimanded, Jed resisted the order from one of Boyd's loyal followers. "How about you leave me alone?" Jed asked and shoved Tuck.

Colton saw the interaction and chuckled.

"What're you laughing at, Indian lover?" Jed asked, getting inches from Colton's face.

"At you being told what to do as if you were a child," Colton replied with a toothy grin.

Jed shoved Colton and said, "Let's step outside and handle this like men."

"I heard you run when someone pulls a gun on you,"

Colton said, laughing.

Tuck returned but grabbed Jed this time by his shoulder and turned him slightly. "Your father won't like this. You're causing trouble again."

Hearing this, Colton suddenly knew who was standing next to him. He turned and asked, "Are you Jed, Boyd's son?"

Too drunk to reason with his ego and pride, nor understand tact, Jed leaned in and hollered, "I am, and I'm also the man who cut that redskin wife of yours open."

Colton's temper went from zero to a hundred. His nostrils flared and his skin got warm.

"You know why I killed her? I wanted to see if her blood was red. You know something, it is," Jed seethed, his front teeth clenched.

Not thinking the situation through and allowing his temper to control his actions, Colton reached for a Bowie knife he kept in the small of his back.

It was all Jed needed. He pulled his pistol, cocked it, and pulled the trigger.

The shot struck Colton in the stomach, causing him to bend over in pain.

The barroom became instantly quiet, and all eyes turned to watch the violent scene play out.

Jed stepped back, cocked the pistol again, and placed the muzzle on the top of Colton's head. "Everyone saw what he did, right? He pulled a knife on me. Look there, he has it in his right hand," Jed cried out, his left hand pointing at Colton's right hand, which hung to his side, the Bowie knife in his grasp.

Colton stood back up. He looked at Jed and barked, "You murdered my beloved wife."

"The only thing I wish I had done before I cut her open was get a little…you-know-what," Jed tormented.

Colton's anger reached a high. He swung the knife at Jed, but was too slow, the shot to the gut was impairing him.

Jed, even in his drunken state, was able to step to the side and avoid the blade.

Colton swung again and once more missed his target.

Not threatened by Colton, Jed laughed. "What's the matter with you?"

Trying again, Colton lashed out. This time his razor-sharp blade hit its mark and slid across Jed's chest. The blade cut through the clothes but only deep enough to leave a scratch.

Shocked that he'd been cut, Jed hollered, "You cut me."

Colton came at him again, but this time Jed was waiting. He stepped to the side and pushed Colton to the floor.

Jed looked down at his chest. He touched it and brought his hand back to find a little blood on it. "Why you Indian-loving son of a bitch!" he screamed.

Knowing what was about to happen, Tuck raced to stop Jed. "No, Jed, don't!"

"Damn you to hell!" Jed hollered and raised his pistol.

Tuck reached Jed in time and slapped the pistol out

of his hand.

"What are you doing?" Jed asked, bewildered.

"Saving your life," Tuck answered.

"From him? He's almost dead," Jed said.

"From your father. Everyone saw he pulled a knife and you defended yourself against that. This though, this could be construed as something else."

"He cut me!" Jed screamed.

"And you shot him. You're even," Tuck said, taking Jed firmly by the arm and escorting him out of the bar forcibly.

Colton rolled around on the floor, clutching his stomach.

"Damn it, someone help the man," the bartender hollered.

Several men picked Colton up off the floor and held him up.

"Take him around back and clean him up," the bartender ordered.

The men dragged Colton around the bar and through a door that led down a short hall to another door, which opened to the back. Outside, they leaned Colton up against a large barrel and left him. Losing blood fast and feeling on the verge of passing out, Colton slid down the barrel and fell to the ground. He looked down at his stomach and laughed when he saw the huge stain of blood on his shirt. "Well, you've done it now, Colton."

Commotion came from inside the bar again.

Colton didn't know what was going on but suspected

it must be Jed again.

The back door burst open, and out came Jed. "Where is he?"

Tuck followed closely behind. "Damn it, Jed, when your father finds out, he's gonna put a hurtin' on ya!"

Jed glared at Tuck and barked, "I'm doing him—hell, I'm doing all of us a favor. By getting rid of him, I'm getting rid of that bounty. With him gone, we can all move forward."

"But now everyone has seen you attack him in the bar. Not everyone in there works for us; we can't control what comes out!" Tuck warned.

"We own this damn town, we own this entire county, and soon when my father is appointed as a senator, we will have power inside the halls of congress," Jed blasted.

Colton laughed.

"What's so damn funny?" Jed asked, his fists clenched in red-hot anger.

"You have no idea, none; it's so beautiful," Colton said, referring to the fact his bounty would still remain but that it would increase to ten thousand in the event he died.

"What am I supposed to tell Marshal Franks when he hears you killed this man in cold blood?"

"You tell him what you want while you give him a sack of money like you always do," Jed answered. He turned back to face Colton and barked, "Pull your gun."

"I don't have one," Colton said, holding up his blood-covered hands.

"Then stand up and pull your knife," Jed ordered,

wanting him to at least try to fight him.

"Don't have that either. Dropped it on the floor in there," Colton said, dropping his arms. His body was growing weak from the loss of blood.

"Give him yours," Jed ordered Tuck.

"What? No. I'm not doing that," Tuck argued.

"Do it, and get him to his feet; then call everyone out here to witness," Jed snapped. Tuck was right that they couldn't control everyone, he knew that, but it could bolster his case for killing him if it looked like a duel.

"You're a damn fool," Tuck roared. He stepped forward, picked up Colton, and leaned him against the barrel.

"Get out here. There's going to be a gunfight!" Jed barked into the bar.

Within seconds the bar emptied out.

Tuck managed to walk Colton over to the right side of the alley. He handed him his Smith & Wesson and ran for cover.

Colton could barely hold the pistol in his hand, and his legs were wobbly. When he looked up, his vision was blurred and his head felt dizzy.

"This man called me out. Now we're going to fight fair and square," Jed cried out to the crowd gathered. "Draw, you low-down Indian lover!" Jed hollered at Colton.

Knowing his fate was now sealed, Colton lifted his head to the sky and said, "I'm coming, my darling, I'm coming." Using what little strength he had left, he raised the pistol.

Jed quickly pulled his pistol from his holster, raising it only to his hip, and fanned the hammer back. A single shot exploded from the muzzle and struck Colton in the chest.

Colton fell backwards like a stiff board. He gasped for air several times, and just before he let out his last breath, he cried out, "I'm comin', darling."

The crowd let out a mixed reaction, some gasping, some clapping and cheering, while others cross talked what they perceived as nothing but murder on the part of Jed.

Jed holstered his Colt and yelled, "Drinks on me."

Regardless of their viewpoints, everyone enjoyed a free drink and quickly assembled back in the bar.

Jed walked over to Colton and spat on his body. "The world is a better place now."

CHAPTER SEVEN

ROCKLAND, IDAHO TERRITORY

AUGUST 31, 1888

Grant needed to pause and set the bushel of potatoes on the ground for fear of dropping them. Never had he felt so weak. It had been over a week since the doc had diagnosed him with lung disease, and ever since he'd been increasingly getting worse, making him wonder if it was all in his head or if he was really deteriorating.

"Let me get that," George said, grabbing the bushel and striding off towards the wagon.

"Here you go, Pa," Margaret said, coming up with a cup full of water.

Grant took the cup and nodded. "Thank you." He gulped it down and handed her back the cup. "It's a fine day, isn't it?" he asked, looking around.

Ignoring his question, Margaret said, "Why don't you come and sit down, take a rest."

"I'm good, I just took my rest. I need to get back at it. Your brother needs the help," Grant said just as George strode by happily to grab another full bushel.

"But you look tired," Margaret said. "I heard you up most of the night coughing."

"Sweetheart, thanks for caring, but these bushels aren't going to load themselves," Grant said.

"Well, if you need anything, just holler," Margaret

said, walking away.

He smiled as he watched her leave. She'd been so good to him since they'd all discovered he was dying from lung disease. Already a doting daughter, she'd increased the tender loving care she gave him, and he appreciated her for it. Whenever the day came for her to marry, that man would be the luckiest man alive; he was just sad knowing he wouldn't be there to see it.

"Pa, someone's coming down the drive," George hollered.

Grant looked up and saw a lone rider racing down his long driveway. Unsure who it was, he made his way from the field towards the house. When he arrived, he discovered it was a post rider.

"Mail for a Grant Toomey," the young post rider said, still riding tall in his saddle.

"That's me," Grant said, holding his hand out.

Margaret exited the house, curious as to what the post might be. She stayed on the front porch and carefully watched the young and, to her, handsome post rider.

The post rider pulled a letter and a small parcel from his satchel and handed them to Grant. "Have a nice day," he said, tipped his hat at Grant and Margaret, then tore off down the drive.

Grant examined the letters and saw one was postmarked from Montana Territory and the other from Sacramento. He ripped open the parcel from Montana. Inside was a folded piece of paper and a gold pocket watch. Upon seeing it, he recognized it as one he had been familiar with years ago. He unfolded the letter and began to read. It was a short, single-paragraph-long letter from an attorney stating that his longtime friend Billy Bartlett was dead, and in his will and testament, he had bequeathed the watch to him. A tinge of sorrow struck him when he reflected that ole Billy was gone, but seeing the watch helped ease that loss. The watch had originally been his, but he'd lost it in a bet to Billy years back. Now after so many years, he had it again.

"What did ya get, Pa?" Margaret asked.

"A watch," Grant said, holding it out for Margaret to see.

She took it and gushed, "It's beautiful."

"It used to be mine. I lost it over a silly wager to a friend, and I just got it back."

"That's nice of him," Margaret said, opening the cover to look at the delicate hands of the watch.

"He was a nice man, but now he's dead."

"Oh, I'm sorry," she said.

"Me too, the letter doesn't say how he died. I suppose old age," Grant said, thinking out loud.

"How else would he die?" Margaret asked.

For men like they had been, there were a variety of ways, but Margaret didn't know they had been bounty hunters and gunmen, so he simply nodded and said, "Old age or sickness."

"Who's the letter from?" Margaret asked.

"I don't know. Why don't you open it up?" Grant said, handing it to her. They so rarely received mail, so being able to open a letter was a special treat.

Margaret happily took it and tore it open. She pulled the several-page note from the envelope and unfolded it. "The handwriting is so beautiful, look," she said, holding it out for Grant to see.

He glanced at it and said, "It is nice handwriting."

Impatient to find out who would send such a beautifully written letter, she began to read. When her eyes hit the word *aunt*, she chirped, "It's from Aunt Ella...she says she and Uncle Benjamin now live in Sacramento...they apologize for not corresponding in such a long time...and that they never came for Mama's funeral and...that they'd love for us to come visit sometime in the future. She goes on to explain that Uncle Ben is now working as a shipping clerk at Union Station, and she has a side job sewing uniforms for the militia garrisoned nearby...she says she loves us, and that's really it," Margaret said.

"I haven't heard from her since you were six," Grant said.

"I can barely remember her," Margaret said, folding the letter back up and sliding it into the envelope.

"Can I have it?" Grant said of the letter.

Margaret handed it to him and asked, "How are you feeling?"

"I'm good," Grant said, putting the letter in his pocket. "Can you take the watch and put it in the secretary along with the letter from the attorney?"

Margaret did what he said and marched off.

A thought suddenly hit him that the timing of Ella's letter was fortuitous. He was dying, and if they needed someone to look after them, he could send them to Sacramento to live with Ella and Ben.

"Pa, I need your help!" George cried from across the field.

Grant shoved the thought aside and headed towards George. Along the way, he stared at him, impressed with the hardworking, strong, vibrant and optimistic young man George had turned into. He could trust that he'd be able to run the farm, but was it fair to straddle him with that responsibility as well as caring for Margaret until she married? He hated that he had to make what felt like rash decisions so quickly.

"Who was that?" George asked when Grant walked up.

"Post rider."

"Anything good?" George asked.

"Found out my old friend died, and Aunt Ella wrote us a letter," Grant answered.

"Who died?"

"A man I knew years ago."

"Who?"

"No one you'd know," Grant replied.

"What did Aunt Ella say? Wait, did she apologize for not coming to Mama's funeral?"

"She did," Grant said.

"I suppose that's positive. Anyway, I need your help tying these down," George said, pointing to the wagonload of full potato bushels.

Grant smiled and said, "Of course, let's get these cinched down and transported into town."

POCATELLO, IDAHO TERRITORY

"Is this how you treat a paying customer?" August hollered as several men tossed him onto the muddy street.

"You haven't paid, that's the issue!" one of the men snapped back. "If we see you in here again, we'll hurt ya real bad!"

Drunk, August struggled to get to his feet. "I'll have you know that I'm only in this Godforsaken town because some son of a bitch murdered my parents, leaving me an orphan," he hollered just before stumbling backwards and falling onto his butt in a puddle. "Damn it."

Just arriving into town, Abigail happened to be riding by and overheard August. She trotted up to him and asked, "Is it true?"

Angry and now covered in wet, cold mud, August yelled, "Is what true?"

"That your parents were murdered?"

August wiped a chunk of mud from his cheek and replied with a gentler tone, "Yes, it's true."

"I heard you say that's the reason you're in Pocatello? Are you looking for their killer?" she asked, finding a curious connection between them.

"I am," August replied, wondering who this young attractive girl was.

"You look the worse for wear. How about you get up and follow me to the hotel down the street? I'll pay for you to get a bath and a hot meal," Abigail offered. Once she said it, she began to wonder where her generosity had come from. It was as if she'd said it without thought, something that was unusual for her. She promptly chalked it up to sympathy for a fellow orphaned traveler.

Managing to finally get to his feet, August asked, "Why would you help me? You don't even know who I am."

"Let's say that I have a tender spot for orphans, being that I am one too. Now come, follow me to the hotel."

"You sure?" August asked, stunned by Abigail's generosity.

"Make up your mind before I change mine," Abigail said, nudging her horse to move forward.

August stumbled ahead, keeping at a slow trot next to her. "You're very nice and…pretty."

Abigail pulled her horse to a stop, sneered at him and said sternly, "Being that you don't know me and I don't know you, I'll give you one chance to make a mistake. First ground rule with me, don't think about calling me pretty or flirting with me. It won't work; in fact, it will do the opposite. Two, if you ever think about laying a hand on me, that will be your last move." She moved her overcoat to the side, allowing him to see her sidearm.

August nodded and said, "Understood."

"Do you have any ground rules?" she asked.

He looked up and thought. "Ahh, nope."

"Then that's really easy," she said.

***

August entered the hotel restaurant. He was washed clean and wearing a fresh set of clothes. His hair was slicked back, his face shaven, and he appeared by his gait to have sobered up a bit.

When Abigail saw him enter the room, she didn't recognize him at first. She waved him over to her table.

He took a seat, looked around at the guests close to them, admiring that he was seated in what appeared to him to be a nice restaurant. "When you travel, do you always stay and eat at hotels?"

"No, I don't. I needed a bath and some supplies. I've been riding for a little over a week," she replied.

"Oh, for a second I thought you must be a wealthy young woman, staying in places like this and all," he said, looking around at the ornately decorated dining room.

"I'm not poor, but I'm not rich," she said.

"You normally wear trousers?" he asked.

"Do you?" she replied.

"Of course, I'm a man," he said.

"And I'm a hu-man. I find them comfortable, and it makes riding a horse a lot easier. I've been known to wear a dress, just for the proper circumstances."

"Hmm, interesting," August said.

"What's your story?" she asked.

"The quick story or the long-winded and soppy version?" he joked.

"Keep it short, please," she answered.

A waiter walked over and handed them a small

menu. "Can I get you something to drink?"

Not waiting for her to respond, August blurted out, "Whiskey."

"Is there a particular brand?" the waiter asked.

"The cheap brand," Abigail replied. "And I'll take a root beer."

"Very well," the waiter said and walked off.

"Root beer?" August quipped.

"I like it; plus I don't like the taste of alcohol," she fired back, nervously shifting the silverware around on the table.

"You don't know what you're missing," he said, his eyes watching her fidget.

"I also like to keep my wits together. I've seen what alcohol can do to a person; that's why I choose not to live that way."

August slid back in his chair and asked, "Let me guess, your father was a drunk?"

She glared at him and said, "I'll take the short story of your life, and be quick about it."

Before he began, he logged a memory that she hadn't responded to his remark about her father. "You kind of know it. I became an orphan eleven years ago after my parents were murdered. I was sent to an orphanage run by sadistic nuns, and two weeks ago or less—I can't quite remember the exact date; it's all been a blur—I was released, and now I'm here sitting with you."

The waiter returned and placed drinks on the table. "Do you wish to order any food?"

"Two steaks and potatoes, thank you," Abigail said,

ordering for both of them.

"Very well," the waiter said, taking the menus and walking away.

"I was looking forward to eating the salmon, but I guess I'll just have to wait," August joked.

"You're welcome, by the way," she said.

"And you, what's your story?" he asked.

"Similar but also not, my mother died giving birth to me. My dad recently died, as did my aunt and uncle. Their deaths were murders though, and I plan on avenging them."

"And that's the part of your story that's similar to mine. I like it, two young adults out for vengeance, almost sounds like a dime novel." August laughed.

"Do you always joke?" she asked, growing annoyed by his personality.

"I prefer to have fun in life. After eleven years under a watchful eye, I'm making up for lost time," he answered.

"Do you know who killed your parents?" she asked.

August leaned in and placed his elbows on the table. "I'd prefer not to share that just yet."

She chuckled and asked, "A bit paranoid, are we?"

"Just that this man is, you could say...well known. I'd hate to have him made aware I was coming for him."

"How do you know he's even alive and where he is?"

"On account I've spent the past few years tracking him down via a couple of Pinkerton detectives I corresponded with. I promised them payment upon my release. I got them to do the work because I fed them a sob story. Anyway, soon they'll realize I've been released and probably come looking for their money. So, who are you out to kill?"

"Like you, I'd rather not say."

"And the murderer is in Idaho?" he asked.

"No, back in Montana. There's a man I need to find that can help me. He used to be a friend of my uncle."

"Where is he?" August asked.

"On a farm outside Rockland, about a day's ride," Abigail said.

August raised his brow and said, "How ironic, the man I'm seeking is in Rockland."

"That is odd. Maybe after I link up with my uncle's friend, we can help you find the man you're looking for," Abigail offered.

"Are you a gun for hire or something?" he asked half-jokingly.

She drank a big gulp of her root beer, wiped the foam from her mouth, and replied, "As a matter of fact, I am."

BIG CIRCLE RANCH, MILES CITY, MONTANA TERRITORY

Once more Boyd found himself pacing his great room in front of an assembly of staff, workers, associates and family.

All gathered watched with bated breath for Boyd to bring down the hammer on Jed. His killing of Colton was the talk of the town and the ranch, causing even Marshal

Franks to take notice and make a call, only to be sent back to Miles City with a fabricated story and gold—exactly as Jed had predicted.

Like before, Jed sat front and center, but this time a smile graced his face. He knew his father would cuss, holler and make threats, but he had cleaned up what his father was incapable of. With Colton out of the way, so was the bounty on his head.

"How many times have I spoken about loyalty?" Boyd crowed, finally breaking the silence. "Huh? Last night I hear that my son was involved in a gunfight with Colton Emery, which resulted in Colton getting killed. I've heard several accounts, one being that my son started the fight, and another that Colton pulled a knife and stabbed Jed, so he was merely defending himself. I can agree with self-defense, I can agree with killing—I can—but not in front of the entire damn town, Jed!"

Jed stood and barked, "He started it in the bar; then it carried outside. We dueled right there in the alleyway for all to see."

"We do things in this family together; we don't go off half-cocked. Tuck tells me he warned you to leave it alone, yet you continued."

"But Marshal Franks is on our side; we'll be fine," Jed declared.

"Marshal Franks is, but the county sheriff isn't, and no doubt upon his return, he'll come around asking questions. I told everyone, including you, to leave Colton Emery alone. Doing anything to him would only bring people snooping, like the county sheriff when he returns from Helena."

"But the bounty, it's gone. We can craft a story around this, and it will be fine. Colton squared off against me and lost, simple as that," Jed said, defending himself.

"Sheriff Johnston is a fair and just man, son. He won't take my money, and he will make sure he gets to the bottom of it. The issue with Martha Emery was one thing, but with you killing Colton, it makes it look suspicious, and you know how I hate people snooping around."

"Then we kill Sheriff Johnston!" Jed roared.

Several in the room gasped at Jed's comment.

"Then what? We kill the next sheriff who wants to investigate?" Boyd replied.

"Father, you're overexaggerating what's happened. We can get past this; we just need to flex our collective muscle," Jed said.

Boyd's nostrils flared and his eyes widened. "Everyone out!"

The group looked around, confused.

"Out!" Boyd hollered.

Not wanting to cross his path, everyone did as he said as fast as they could.

"Except you. You stay," Boyd said to Jed.

When the room emptied, Boyd walked over to Jed and stood inches from his face. "I've done nothing but flex what muscles I have to grow this ranch to the largest in the territory. I've even gone as far as to leverage the influence we have to ensure that I don't just create wealth for me, but for generations to come. This is not about me or you, but our legacy, and your childish antics could destroy it all."

"Since when are you against killing our enemies?"

"I'm not, I just don't do it in public," Boyd said.

"Well, maybe it's time we change that," Jed fired back. He had a renewed defiance that was startling.

Boyd raised his finger and waved it in front of Jed's face. "This is your last chance."

"Or what?"

"Just know that. No more chances. I'll do my best to clean this up one last time," Boyd said, walking away from Jed.

"I'm so sorry I'm a disappointment to you," Jed quipped.

Boyd shot him a spiteful look then called out, "Clement, get in here."

Clement, who had been just on the other side of the door, raced inside, "Yes, Mr. Wallace."

"Pass the word around, no one is allowed in town until I say otherwise, and keep your ear to the ground, as the bounty hunters will be coming in droves, no doubt."

"What bounty hunters? There isn't a bounty anymore!" Jed mocked.

"Son, you're a fool. The bounty is still there. Colton had the money placed in a holding account with specific instructions."

"What? He can't do that," Jed whined.

"He can and he did. And you should know that now the mystery of who did it is gone. Oh, and he increased it to ten thousand."

"How do you know this?" Jed asked.

"You never listen, son; I know everything, I hear everything," Boyd said. He faced Clement and continued, "Beef up security around the perimeter of the homestead, and I repeat, no one is allowed to go into town unless I approve."

"Yes, sir."

Jed stood wallowing in the fact the bounty was still on his head.

Boyd gave Jed one last look, shook his head in disgust, and left the room.

After his father left, Jed clenched his teeth and growled under his breath, "I hate you."

POCATELLO, IDAHO TERRITORY

Patting his belly, August leaned back in the dining room chair and burped. "That was great."

Maintaining proper etiquette, Abigail dabbed her lips with the napkin and placed the knife and fork on the plate in a manner that told the waiter she was done.

"Say, where in Montana are you heading after you find this person in Rockland?" August asked, reaching for what was his third glass of whiskey.

"Miles City," she answered.

August coughed when he heard the name of the town. "I've heard about that town recently, but where?" he asked himself out loud.

"It's a no-nothing place in eastern Montana; surprised you would have heard of it," Abigail said.

He pressed his eyes closed and thought. After pausing for a while, he opened his eyes wide with excitement and blurted out, "Now I know. Back in Fort Collins, a bartender mentioned it. He said someone is offering a sizeable bounty up there."

"You heard about the bounty for Martha Emery all the way down in Fort Collins?" she asked, surprised that news like that had traveled so far.

"When a bounty is that size, word travels fast," he said, waving the waiter over.

The waiter rushed over and asked, "What can I get for you?"

Not wanting to pay for another drink, Abigail interrupted and said, "The check, we're finished."

August glared at her and said, "Speak for yourself."

"Drink all you want, but not on my dime," she shot back.

The waiter watched them spar then pulled out a small slip of paper and handed it to August. "The bill."

Annoyed by the sexism, Abigail reached over and snatched the bill from August's hand. "Now why would you think he was paying?" she asked the waiter.

"On account he's the gentleman, ma'am," the waiter answered.

"He may be a man, but I'm paying. This sad sap doesn't have two pennies to press together." Abigail laughed.

"Pardon me, ma'am," the waiter said just before he walked off.

"After I finish with my business in Rockland, I'm

heading to Miles City to collect that bounty," August said.

Abigail counted a couple of coins and set them on the table. She looked up at August and asked, "You're going to try to find the killer or killers?"

"What else am I going to do to make money? Plus that bounty is huge; if I score that, I'll be set for a while," August said.

"Have you ever hunted a man before?" she asked.

"No, but how hard can it be?" he asked in a mocking tone.

"It can be hard," she said.

"Say, maybe we can ride together to Rockland and help each other; then head to Miles City and work as, say, a team to get that bounty?" August asked.

"I don't know you. Why would I ride with someone I just met?" she asked. "Plus it's an easy ride. If I head out in the early morning, I'll make Rockland by late afternoon or earlier. It's about twenty miles southwest."

"You ride with people for company and safety, that's why," he answered.

She chewed on the idea for a mere second. "No, I will be fine."

"Come on, why not?" he asked. His motivation to ride with her was mainly rooted in the fact she appeared to have money.

She stood up and said, "August, it was nice meeting you, but this is where we go our own ways."

He shrugged his shoulders and asked, "Why?"

"You have nothing, and it appears to me you're a drunk. I'm open to a partner, but I need someone with experience and discipline."

"Oh, I see, you're too good for me?"

"As a matter of fact, I am," she said and walked off.

He jumped up and followed her to the stairs. "Hold on."

Being polite, she stopped and said, "No."

"At least think about it," he urged.

"Good night, August, and you're welcome for the meal," she quipped.

"Yes, thank you, sorry; and please reconsider."

As she ascended the stairs, she said, "Good night and have a nice life."

August wasn't one for accepting a simple no. Determined to get his way, he'd just have to find a way to convince her.

CHAPTER EIGHT

ROCKLAND, IDAHO TERRITORY

SEPTEMBER 1, 1888

It had taken Abigail less time than she thought to ride the last remaining twenty miles to Rockland. However, getting there was half the trip; now she needed to find where Grant actually resided. Using her instincts, she rode into the small town and began asking around; soon enough she was given directions to the Toomey farm, which lay a mile and a half outside town.

She arrived at the end of the driveway but paused before riding down it. She saw the house in the distance but didn't see anyone outside.

With only a few hours of light left in the day, she brushed aside her misgivings about showing up at Grant's house uninvited and prayed he'd give her the time of day. She nudged her horse and raced down the drive. When she stopped just outside the front of the house, she looked around for anyone outside but still didn't see anyone. Were they not home? she asked herself.

The clack of the front door latch told her she was wrong.

She looked and saw the door open then a girl step out. It was Margaret.

"Can I help you?" Margaret asked.

Nervous, she thought for a second, making sure she

used the correct name, and said, "I'm here to see Grant Toomey."

"He's inside," Margaret said.

"Can you get him, please?" Abigail asked, still riding tall in the saddle.

"He's resting. I don't think he's up for any visitors. Does it have something to do with the farm? If it does, my brother, George, can help," Margaret said.

"What's wrong with him?" Abigail asked, concerned upon hearing Grant was sick.

"He's just under the weather. Can I ask who you are?"

"My name is Abigail Bartlett. Tell him that, please. It's urgent I speak to him," Abigail said.

Seeing the look of urgency in her face and tone, Margaret said, "I'll go see if he's awake and let him know you're here. Would you care for a glass of lemonade?"

"You wouldn't happen to have root beer, would ya?" Abigail asked, dismounting the horse. She walked it over and lashed the reins to a post.

"No root beer. If you'll excuse me, I'll be right back," Margaret said then disappeared into the house.

Abigail walked around the front of the house, admiring the flowers and plants in the bed off the deck, taking a special liking to the small white flowers.

"Those are called snow-in-summer," George said, walking up behind her.

Abigail spun around, a look of surprise on her face. "Oh, hi. Um, they're beautiful."

"My mother planted them years ago. You'll find

them all over the farm," George said, wiping his dirty hands on a rag.

The front door opened, and out stepped Grant. He looked right at Abigail and asked, "Are you Billy Bartlett's daughter?"

"No, sir, I'm his niece, but Uncle Billy was like a father to me," Abigail said.

"I heard about him. I'm sorry," Grant said, stepping off the porch and walking up to her.

"Thank you."

"Is that why you're here, to tell me?" Grant asked.

"Yes, but how did you know already?" Abigail asked.

"I received a parcel with a letter from an attorney in town. It said he was dead, and he returned a watch he'd won from me years ago," Grant said, pulling the gold watch from his pocket and showing it to her.

Seeing the watch made Abigail's heart sink. She remembered the watch intimately. It seemed out of place in Grant's hands. "I know that watch. I remember it quite well."

"He said he'd give it back to me. It was a promise made and a promise kept," Grant said proudly, thinking of his old friend.

Her eyes longingly looked at the watch.

Grant noticed her gaze and asked, "Do you want to see it?"

"Oh, no, no, that's fine," she lied.

He put the watch back in his pocket and said, "I'm sorry you made that long trip to tell me something I already knew."

"I did come to tell you he was dead but also to tell you that his death was murder. Both he and Aunt Nell were murdered, shot in cold blood," Abigail confided.

Grant's eyes bulged. "What?"

"Yes, I witnessed it with my own eyes."

Grant looked at George, who was listening intently, and ordered, "Go clean up for dinner."

"But I want to hear what happened to her uncle," George whined.

"Inside," Grant ordered George. He turned to Margaret and said, "You too, finish dinner; set an extra place setting for Abigail."

"Yes, Pa," Margaret said then walked back inside the house.

George followed Margaret.

When the door closed, Grant motioned with his head and said, "Walk with me."

The two walked towards the barn. Abigail explained in greater detail what had happened that night, with Grant simply listening. When they reached the edge of the barn, Grant asked, "What happened to your uncle is tragic, a crime; what I want to know is why you're here telling me and not the local law?"

"On account the local authorities work for the men who killed them. Also, my uncle Billy told me about you; said you were a notorious bounty hunter, a real gunman."

"I see, I know what you want," Grant said, nodding.

"I need you to come with me and avenge my uncle's and aunt's murders," Abigail said.

"I'm very sorry about what happened to them,

believe me I am, but the days of me killin' people is over. I gave that all up many years ago—seventeen years to be exact."

"Please, I'd do it myself, but I need someone with your experience who can help me, show me how to do it," Abigail pleaded.

"I know as a matter of fact that Billy would not want you doing this. I'm sure he's rolling in his grave right now."

"You need to come back with me. I need to do this," Abigail said.

"Even if I wanted to, I can't right now; I need to focus on how to take care of my kids. I'm dying, and I need to find seven hundred dollars to pay the territorial government by late October or I lose the farm."

Abigail turned away, clearly upset by Grant's unwillingness to help.

"I'm truly sorry. Plus you wouldn't want me anymore. I'm sick. I'd be more of a hindrance," Grant said, placing his hand on her shoulder.

"There's a bounty for the man who killed Uncle Billy," she said, turning around and offering the nugget that could persuade him.

"No bounty will help with what I need. How much could a bounty for Billy be? Heck, the bounty for Jesse James was five thousand, and that was for one of the most famous outlaws known," Grant said.

"It's seven thousand," Abigail blurted out.

Grant's eyes widened. "Seven thousand? What? There's no way."

"Yes, seven thousand. The man that killed Uncle Billy and Aunt Nell murdered another woman. Her husband used to be a successful merchant; he's placed the bounty," Abigail said. "If you'll come with me, I'll show you." Abigail marched towards her horse.

"Hold on," Grant said, motioning for her to stay.

Stubborn, Abigail didn't listen. She got to her horse, opened a saddlebag, and rummaged through it. After she found what she was looking for, she pulled it out and hollered, "Right here."

Grant hadn't followed her; he'd stayed put for fear George or Margaret would overhear the conversation. "Come back here."

Abigail did as he asked, handing him the folded poster when she arrived. "It says it right there."

Grant unfolded it and read. He was in shock at the value. "I'm sure there are dozens of bounty hunters converging on Miles City."

"But no one knows who really did it. I do."

"You're telling me no one knows who the killer of this woman is but you?" Grant asked.

"Correct."

Grant turned away from her and started to pace. "Seven thousand would pay the fee and leave a lot of money for improvements, acquisitions. It would save the farm and give the kids the cushion they need after I'm dead."

"I was thinking we could split it," Abigail confessed.

"Then the bounty is only thirty-five hundred?"

"There's talk now that it's been raised to ten

thousand," Abigail said, trying to sweeten the pot.

"But that's just hearsay, right?" he asked.

"Yes," she confessed regretfully.

"Listen, kid—"

"I'm not a kid. I just turned eighteen," Abigail countered.

"Listen, little lady, like I said, I can't really be leaving my children during this time," Grant said.

"You said you needed the money. How about if I gave you two-thirds? Would that be enough to convince you to come, on top of you helping avenge your friend's murder?"

"I gave my word to my wife years ago that I was done with that life. I can't go back on that promise because I'm in need of money."

"But it's more than money, it's about saving your farm; I imagine your wife would want you to do that," Abigail said, standing with her arms folded.

Grant looked up at the house and could see George peering out the window. "Let's go get dinner. I imagine you're hungry and tired. You can stay here tonight. I'll get Margaret to set you up."

"I am hungry," Abigail said.

"Come, let's get you fed," Grant said and escorted her to the house.

CHAPTER NINE

ROCKLAND, IDAHO TERRITORY

SEPTEMBER 2, 1888

Abigail emerged from the spare room after a restful sleep to disappointment, as she found the kitchen empty. With only a candle to light her way, she made her way around the small space, looking for something to eat. She'd been fed to her fill the night before but woke with hunger pangs. What she was hoping to find was a piece of the bread she'd had with dinner. Margaret had called it sourdough, it was the first time she'd ever had it, and she woke craving it.

Adjacent to the oven she spotted a shelf, and on it was a covered basket. "I wonder," she mused and walked over to it. She opened the lid and hovered the candle over it to find half a loaf of the bread. "Yes," she chirped. She removed the bread and set it on the table. She looked around and said, "If I were a knife, I'd be?"

"You can just rip off a piece too," Grant said from the hall.

Abigail jumped and said, "You scared me. I'm sorry, I was hungry."

"Don't apologize. I couldn't sleep, and when I heard someone out here, I thought it might be you, so I thought it might be a good time to chat."

Curious as to what he wanted to discuss but still

craving the bread, she pulled a chunk of the moist center from the loaf and stuffed it into her mouth.

"You must be really hungry," he joked.

Covering her mouth, she said, "Was that rude?"

Taking a seat at the table, he motioned with his hand not to worry. "I do that all the time. Please help yourself."

Taking him up on that, she tore another piece of bread off and took a bite. "This is so good."

"It's better with butter," Grant said, getting up and grabbing a covered jar and returning to the table. He set it on the table and took a small butter knife from a basket and placed it next to the jar.

She uncovered the jar to find butter. With the knife she scooped out a bit and slathered the piece of bread with it. Her mouth watered when she looked at the piece then took a bite. "Mmm, so good," she said with a smile. She licked her fingers and took a seat across from him.

"I've been thinking about what happened to Billy and Nell, as well as the job. Let me ask you a question, and I need you to be honest with me," he said.

"Okay."

"If I say no, what will you do?" he asked.

"I plan on going back and killing Jed Wallace then collecting that bounty," she answered.

"Even if I don't go with you, that's what you're going to do?" he asked.

"Yes."

"Billy wouldn't want you to do that," he said.

"Don't matter, I'm going to do it. You should have seen it. They murdered them, both of them, for nothing, all because we had discussed the bounty."

"Wait, he was killed because this Jed Wallace knew you had talked about it?"

"Something like that. All Uncle Billy was doing was playing around. He liked to talk about his days riding with you, and he wanted to show me how you two would gather information."

"I see, that got back to this Jed, and he had them killed."

"He would have killed me too if I hadn't escaped. But you should know Uncle Billy's murder was no doubt ordered by Jed's father, Boyd Wallace."

"Hold on, hold on. Boyd Wallace, the Boyd Wallace of the Big Circle Ranch?" Grant asked. He had heard of Boyd before.

"You know him?"

"Everyone knows Boyd Wallace, so this Boyd is what relation to Jed?"

"Jed is his son."

"This raises the stakes. You can't go back there by yourself."

"Then that means you're coming with me?" she asked.

"No, you're staying here, where you're safe. Billy would want that. We have the room; you can live here. You need a home; now you have it."

"No!" she barked.

"Keep your voice down," Grant snapped back.

"I won't be told what to do, I'm an adult now, and I won't be bossed around. Here's the deal, Mr. Toomey,

Tillis, whatever your name is. I'm going back to Miles City, and I'm going to kill Jed Wallace, and I'm collecting that bounty with or without you," she said, standing up from the table and walking off.

"Abigail, wait a second," he called out.

She stopped and turned around. "Unless you're about to say you're coming with me, I don't want to hear it."

"Abigail, please come back, and let's talk about this," he said.

"No."

Without warning, Grant began to cough loudly. His body tensed with every cough, and his eyes began to tear from the violent coughs.

Noticing how bad his coughing was, Abigail came over and rubbed his back. "Can I get you anything?"

He pointed to a cloth napkin next to the water basin and waved, signaling he wanted her to bring it to him.

She grabbed it and gave it to him.

He placed it over his mouth and began to hack loudly. As fast as his cough had come on, it subsided. He pulled the napkin away from his mouth to see thick blood on it.

Abigail saw the blood and asked, "What do you have?"

"Lung disease, I'm dying," he said.

"Sorry."

"Me too." Grant laughed. "Hey, you should go get some more sleep. If you're leaving when the sun comes up, you'll need it."

Unsure what to say after witnessing his coughing fit, she sauntered back to her room and closed the door.

Grant again looked at the blood. It was a reminder that his death was not far off and that he didn't have long to find a solution to the farm and his children's future. The thought of going out for a job had seemed impossible just the day before; now he was seriously considering it. If he did go, no matter if he returned or not, it would be his last ride.

***

Her early morning snack and chat with Grant caused Abigail to sleep longer than she had planned. When she finally opened her eyes, she discovered the sun was up, and by the sounds coming from outside, the day had started for everyone else.

She tossed off the blanket, got her clothes on, and exited the room. This time she found Margaret in the kitchen.

"Good morning," Margaret said with a pleasant smile.

"Oh, hi, good morning," Abigail said, rushing past with her saddlebags slung over her shoulder. She exited the house and froze when she saw Grant standing between her horse and another. "What are you doing?"

"What does it look like?" he asked, loading up a saddlebag on his horse.

"Are you coming with me?" she asked.

Grant cinched the bag tight and walked over to her.

"I thought about everything you said. First, I can't let you go alone; two, I need the money; and three, it's the right thing bringing Billy and Nell's killer to justice."

"I'm not bringing them to justice, I'm killing them."

"That's where we differ."

"It's not your choice, and I'm not asking you to do it, I am," she declared.

"How about we agree to disagree on that point? We'll discuss it on the ride to Miles City. I estimate it'll take us about two weeks to get there. I've packed some extra grain and corn for the horses so we can keep a steady pace."

"Two weeks? It took me less than that to get here," Abigail protested.

"And you're lucky you didn't kill your horse. I stick to about forty miles per day, sometimes a bit more, but over the years I found that was a good day's ride," Grant said.

"What did you tell Margaret and George?" she said just above a whisper, her eyes scanning to see if George was close by.

"I haven't told them just yet," Grant said.

"But you're...the horse?" she asked, confused, as he was there loading up his horse.

"You get your stuff situated, and I'll go talk to them," he said. He turned and called out, "George, come to the house. We need to talk."

"Be right there, Pa," George hollered from the barn.

Grant winked at Abigail and went into the house.

George dashed from the barn, sprinted past Abigail,

ensuring he gave her a wave and a smile, then darted into the house.

Margaret and Grant were already at the table waiting.

"Pa, are you going somewhere?" George asked, pulling a chair out and taking a seat.

Grant cleared his throat and gave each of them a nervous look. "We all know I'm dying, and we all know we need to come up with seven hundred dollars in less than two months or we lose the farm."

"I told ya, we'll figure it out," George said confidently.

"You were right, I have figured it out, but it requires that I leave today with Abigail and head to Miles City, Montana."

"What's there?" Margaret asked.

Grant lowered his head and sighed. "I promised I'd be honest with you, so I'm going to now. I don't know how you're going to take this, but the truth is important, it's important you know who your father really is."

"What does that mean?" Margaret asked. "Who is Abigail?"

"She's a niece of an old friend of mine, you know that already, but that friend of mine, Billy Bartlett, he and I used to work together years back before you two were born and even before I met your mother."

"So everything else you told us was a lie?" George asked.

"Thing is, I never did that. The truth is I was a bounty hunter," Grant blurted out.

Margaret's eyes widened with shock.

George's jaw dropped but an almost gleeful chirp burst from his mouth. "Really? Like a real bounty hunter?"

"Yes, and I was good at it, too good. I gave it all up when I met your mother. She changed my life, set me on the path to be a better man, the man that I am today, your father. I couldn't have been your father if I still lived that life. I had to let that man go," he said. He then began to contemplate if he should tell them his real name but decided against it. There was no value for them knowing that detail.

"You are serious. This isn't a joke," Margaret said, her expression showing she was still in shock at the revelation.

"It's true," Grant confessed.

"Why did you never tell us?" she asked.

"On account that the man who did that was gone; he was dead to me. I let him go many years ago."

"Wow, a bounty hunter," George cooed.

"Abigail is going to collect a bounty, and she needs my help. I can't let her go alone, Billy would do the same if you needed help, and I need to help her. She's all alone in this world, and I owe him that," Grant said.

"Is this dangerous? This seems dangerous," Margaret asked.

"It will be, or I should say, it could be," Grant answered.

"No, you can't go. I feel bad for her, but you can't leave," Margaret said, her body tense and stiff.

"I have to, we need the money, and the bounty is

substantial. It's enough to pay the fee and give you both a future when I'm gone. The fact is I'm dying. I may not live two months, it's true. This is my chance to get the money we need to keep the farm and set you up to expand the operation here."

"I won't allow it. You can't leave," Margaret said, slapping her hand on the table.

Grant reached out and touched her hand. "Sweetheart, please, I can't leave with you upset like this. I need your blessing."

Tears streamed down her cheeks. "What if you don't return?"

"I may not," he said honestly.

"Then I won't give you my blessing."

"Marg, we need the money, and Pa is right; this might be our chance," George said.

"Don't side with him," she snapped at George.

"If I don't go, Abigail will go alone, and she'll most certainly die. I can't let that happen. I'm good at this; I used to be one of the best."

"Did you ever kill anyone?" George asked. He leaned in and anxiously waited for the answer.

"That has no bearing on right now," Grant replied.

"You did," George said. He gave Margaret a look and said, "Pa has killed people. Oh my God, my father is a bounty hunter, a gunslinger."

"Stop acting the fool, George," Margaret wailed, her sadness turning to anger.

"Margaret, I need to go. It's the right thing to do. Abigail needs me, and I need to save the farm."

"Then go, leave," Margaret barked. She tore from her chair and ran to her room, slamming the door behind her.

"Want me to check on her?" George asked.

"No, I've got it," Grant said, rising and going to her bedroom door. He knocked and said, "Margaret, please open up."

"Go away."

"Margaret, please."

Pitter-patter on the floor sounded; then the door unlocked.

Grant opened the door and stepped in. "I need your blessing, please."

"Why do you need it? I'm just a child," she cried.

"You're more than a child. You're so much more. You're becoming a beautiful young woman. You're so mature, smart, wise beyond your years, responsible. I love you deeply, but I also respect you, and having you say yes will make my trip easier."

"Then, yes," she blared.

"I need you to mean it. Look at me," Grant said, tenderly touching her arm.

She looked at him and softly asked, "What happens if I never see you again?"

That question made his heart hurt. He looked into her deep blue eyes and said, "I'll always be with you, just like your mama has always been with you. I'm right there and there," he said, pointing at her chest then her head.

"Oh, Pa, I love you so much, I don't want you to go, but I know we need to save this farm. This is my home and the one thing I need after you're gone. If I lose you, then it, I don't know what I'll do," she wailed just before embracing him.

He held her tight and said, "I love you, baby girl. You're the most precious thing to me. I have been so blessed to have you as my daughter. Believe me when I say leaving now to go to do this job is the last thing I want to do. I'd rather stay with you until I leave this world, but for some reason God has chosen this path. First it was the fee; now this girl shows up in need. I have to go."

"Then let me give you a bunch of food for your ride. You can't go without food," she said, jumping up from her bed and racing out of the room towards the kitchen.

Grant joined her there.

She packed a basket and said, "Put this in your saddlebag for the ride."

Tears came to his eyes. "I love you."

"I love you too, Pa."

He exited the house to find Abigail standing next to her horse, talking to George. "I've got more food for the trip."

"Good, and thank you," Abigail said, giving a nod to Margaret.

"You watch out for my pa," Margaret said.

"I will," Abigail said.

Grant gave George a hug and said, "Take care of your sister. She's the gem of this family."

"So what does that make me?" George asked.

"You're now the rock," Grant answered, patting him

on the shoulder.

Grant and Abigail mounted their horses.

Abigail tipped her hat and said, "Thank you for everything." She nudged her horse and began to trot off.

Grant gave his kids one last look and said, "I'll see you soon." He pulled the reins hard and turned the horse towards the drive and trotted away.

Margaret grasped George's arm and said, "Look closely."

"Why?" George asked.

"Because this is the last time we'll ever see Pa again."

CHAPTER TEN

NORTH OF EAGLE ROCK, IDAHO TERRITORY

SEPTEMBER 3, 1888

In his arm, Grant cradled kindling and some larger branches back to the campfire.

The deep orange glow illuminated Abigail working on dinner. Laid out on a tanned leather hide, she was busy skinning a groundhog, or what was better known in those parts as a whistle pig.

Seeing what she was doing, Grant said, "I haven't eaten one of those varmints in years." He tossed the wood on the ground next to the fire.

"I don't think they taste too bad. I take peppercorn and grind it up; then along with some salt, I rub it on the flesh then cook it," Abigail said as she slid a metal rod through the body the long way so she could create a spit.

"Well, I look forward to trying it," Grant said, taking a seat next to his bedroll.

She winked at him and quipped, "I'm a fabulous cook. You'll love it."

"I'll take your word for it," he said. "So what happened to your parents?"

"Both dead," she replied.

"How? Sickness, disease?" he asked.

"I killed them," she said with a devilish grin.

He cocked his head and asked, "Serious?"

Looking up from what she was doing, she answered, "Yes. I killed them both. My mother died giving birth to me, and I shot my father."

"Wait, you shot your father?" Grant asked, shocked to hear her response.

"Don't start regretting your decision to come with me. Uncle Billy approved of the killing. My father was a mean and evil man. He got what was coming to him."

"Did he used to hurt you?" Grant asked.

"Every day. He wasn't a reliable person. Never knew if we were going to have food or if there'd be wood for the fire; but one thing was certain, he'd beat on me every day."

"I'm glad you shot him," Grant said.

She went back to setting up the spit and said, "I'm glad you approve."

Branches cracked feet away from their campsite.

Abigail drew her pistol quickly and spun in the direction of the noise.

Grant wasn't as fast as she was but had his old Colt in hand a couple of seconds later. "Who's there?"

With his arms high, August emerged from the darkness. "Hi, Abigail."

"August, you could have gotten shot," she barked as she holstered her pistol.

"You know him?" Grant asked, wary of August. There was something he saw in his face he instantly didn't trust.

August grinned and gave a cautious eye to Grant.

"What are you doing here?" she asked.

"I, um," he stuttered.

"Have you been following me?" she asked before looking at Grant. "Us?"

August stepped closer to the fire and answered, "I knew if I could talk to you again, I could convince you to take me with you."

"That bounty won't split three ways, at least my part won't," Grant said, interjecting himself into the conversation and establishing he was in control.

"I don't think that's up to you, old man," August growled, tossing aside the initial timid approach and replacing it with his usual cockiness.

"As a matter of fact, I do. Now why don't you keep moving along," Grant said.

Abigail looked at Grant and noticed he hadn't put his pistol away just yet; he was still holding it but had it in his lap. Not wanting the situation to deteriorate, she said, "August, you're more than welcome to have dinner with us."

"I think I will," August said, lowering himself to the ground and crisscrossing his legs.

"Who is he?" Grant asked.

"I met him in Pocatello. He lost his parents; both were murdered," Abigail replied. She picked up a stick and was now poking the hot coals of the fire with it.

"Who are you?" August asked Grant.

"My name is Grant."

"Hi, Grant, my name is Augustus, but you can call me August."

"Mr. Toomey is the man I went to find in Rockland.

He's coming with me to Miles City to get the bounty," Abigail said.

"Grant Toomey, huh?" August said, sneering at Grant.

"Listen, kid, you can get up and just leave if you're going to sit in my camp and stare at me like that."

"Okay, old man," August said.

"I am old and grumpy; you don't want to see me when I get grumpy," Grant joked.

"You boys, just calm down. Grant here is an old friend of my uncle's, and I need him. And, Grant, August here means well; he's just been through a lot like me. Oh, that reminds me. Did you manage to get to Rockland yourself and find the man you were looking for?"

August smiled at Abigail and said, "I found him."

"And?" she asked.

"Abby, how about we have a more civil conversation than talk like that, alright?" he asked.

She nodded.

"Who were you looking for in Rockland?" Grant asked, curious.

"Like I told her, I don't want to talk about it. But what I do want to talk about is that bounty," August said.

"You're not riding with us," Grant blurted out. "It's only seven thousand, and I'm not giving up any of my share for a third person."

"It's ten now," August said.

"That's rumor," Grant countered.

"I heard on good authority it's ten," August said.

"Whatever it is, ten or seven, I get a percentage, and

my percentage isn't paying for a third party," Grant said, being stubborn.

"I'm going for the bounty with or without you two, so we can share it, or I can leave here and get there before you two and secure it myself," August threatened.

Hearing those words, Grant perked up. If August was serious, and he had no reason to doubt him, then they'd be competing with him.

"Mr. Toomey doesn't like to ride with people he doesn't know, and I have to agree," Abigail said, the glow of the fire dancing off her skin.

"Then this is where I bid you farewell, fellow travelers. When we meet again in Miles City, I'll have that bounty all to myself," August said, standing. He dusted off his trousers and tipped his hat to Abigail.

"Wait," Grant said.

August turned to face Grant and grinned. "Yes."

"Abby and I already have an agreement. I'm getting two-thirds—"

August interrupted him, as he had quickly calculated what his share might be, "Don't bother finishing talking. I'm not doing this for a little over eleven hundred dollars. We split it three ways, period."

"If you let me finish, I was going to say that I'll take only sixty percent—"

"Fifty-five," August fired back.

Grant stewed for a second then relented. "Fifty-five percent, you two split the remaining."

August shot a look at Abigail.

She was staring at Grant, shocked that he had made a

deal with August. "Are you sure?"

"Yes," Grant said.

"Well?" August asked Abigail.

She gave August a glance and said, "Welcome to the team, August."

BIG CIRCLE RANCH, MILES CITY, MONTANA TERRITORY

Boyd hovered over a large table in his office. On it sat a map of Montana. On the right side of the map a red line sectioned off part of it. Just above it, red hash marks carved out another part. His finger followed the red hash marks along until they stopped at the solid red line. He stood, picked up a glass half full of scotch, and said, "Job well done, Boyd." Tapping on his office door tore him away. He called out, "Who is it?"

"It's Jed, Father."

"Come on in," Boyd barked.

Jed walked into the office. He looked around the dimly lit room; only the roaring fireplace and a single kerosene lantern illuminated the space. "Do you have a few minutes to talk?"

Boyd looked at a clock on the mantel and said, "I have exactly a few minutes. Come on in; take a seat at the fireplace."

Jed smiled and hurried into the room. He sat down in one of two wingback chairs that were placed facing each other in front of the fireplace.

"Want a drink?" Boyd offered.

"Sure."

Boyd poured Jed a glass then filled his. He walked over and handed Jed a glass. After Jed took it, Boyd tapped it and said, "Cheers, son. I'm glad you're here. I have some good news."

Jed took a big gulp and asked, "What's the news?"

"That two-thousand-plus-acre parcel to the north, I just acquired it," Boyd said proudly, leaning back in his chair.

"Congratulations, Father," Jed said before putting the glass to his lips and taking another large gulp.

"Slow down, Jed, that's forty-year-old scotch. You're not supposed to drink it like that rotgut at the Elk's Head."

Jed gave Boyd a nervous smile and said, "Sorry."

"What is it you'd like to talk about?" Boyd asked.

"The operation you have in Arizona, the mining operation, I'd like you to give it to me," Jed said.

Boyd chuckled.

"I'm serious, Father. I think I'm ready to run something on my own, and I'd like to run that," Jed said.

"Jed, my boy, those mines produce for me. I can't have some nitwit take charge," Boyd said.

"I'm not a nitwit," Jed barked.

"Son, I love you, but you just don't have the temperament to run an operation like that. Look, maybe I can put you in charge of a team up here running some cattle."

"I don't want to run a team up here. I want the mining operation in Arizona."

"Well, you're not going to get that," Boyd said, leaning in. "I just had to whip you in front of the entire ranch to show people that I mean what I say. I had to use my own son as an example that no one gets a free pass. I can't now turn around and give you an operation like Arizona, but like I said, let me talk with Clement or Tuck about one of the cattle teams."

Jed gripped the glass tightly in his hand and clenched his jaw.

"I see you're upset. You should go, get some rest; think about taking over one of the cattle teams," Boyd said calmly, patting Jed's knee.

Angry, Jed stood and threw the empty glass into the fireplace. "I hate you!"

Boyd leaned back in his chair and smiled. "And this is why I don't let you take over an operation like Arizona."

"You've treated me like this my entire life!" Jed hollered. "Treating me like a child. You had me whipped like I was some common ranch hand!"

"Because you are a common ranch hand who also happens to be my son. And the reason I treat you like a child is because you act like one."

Jed took an aggressive step towards Boyd, his fist clenched.

"I'd suggest you stop right there, because the next thing you do could be your last," Boyd said, pulling out a large Bowie knife. He held it up; the long nine-inch blade glimmered in the light of the fireplace.

Jed halted his advance; a look of fear gripped him.

Boyd stood and stepped up to within inches of Jed. He placed the flat part of the blade against Jed's crotch and tapped. "I should cut you from your balls to your sternum and gut you like a deer."

"Father, I was merely upset. I thought—"

"Just shut your mouth. Your mother has spoiled you, telling you from day one that you can do or be just by thinking about it. The problem is she forgot to tell you the biggest part is that you have to work and act a certain way to get it. You can't just think your way to something, you have to act, do, and that takes a man of action and patience because great things don't come instantly, they come from time and effort spent. Son, your head is all messed up. You somehow think that what I've created is somehow yours, it's not; none of this is yours. Have I shared some of it with you because you're my son? Of course, but don't think you can do or get what you want just because you are my son; you need to earn it."

"Yes, Father."

"Here's what's going to happen. I'm going to send you and your friend Edward off to the north end, to Purgatory, to start working on fencing and marking our newest acquisition…" Purgatory was the name of an old hunting cabin that Boyd used to use; it had been abandoned for many years now.

"But—"

"Shut…your…mouth," Boyd growled.

Jed lowered his head and listened.

"You'll leave in the morning and won't return until you're done that job. I'll have Clement or Tuck make sure you get all the provisions you'll need minus liquor because I need your head clear, I need you to start thinking. I estimate that it'll take you about a month or so to complete your work up there. Now, what I want to see upon your return is a new person come through these doors, not one believing they're entitled but one who is grateful, even grateful for the work of fencing. You see, son, a man that takes pride in work and is thankful to have employment is a man I want working for me and one that can advance. Do I make myself clear?"

Jed nodded.

"Now go, pack what you'll need for the trip. You'll leave first thing in the morning."

CHAPTER ELEVEN

BILLINGS, MONTANA TERRITORY

SEPTEMBER 6, 1888

The past three days of riding had taken a toll on Grant. He was out of shape for this sort of travel, and with his lung disease adding a heavy layer of fatigue, it was making the trip worse. However, Grant was the sort of man that when he needed to get somewhere, he wouldn't quit. When he woke that morning, he told Abigail and August to saddle up and be ready for a tough ride. His plan was to push the horses, transitioning between cantering and galloping the sixty plus miles it would take to get to Billings. There he told them they'd trade their horses in for new ones and keep pressing forward after resting. The plan of doing forty miles per day just wasn't going to happen anymore. He could feel the lung disease getting worse, and if he was going to get to Miles City, get Jed Wallace, and return to see his children, he needed to pick up the pace.

When he saw the sign welcoming them to Billings, he let out a sigh of relief.

August had been keeping his eye on Grant for the past three days. It didn't take an expert to see Grant was ill.

Grant took them to the first livery he found.

A young man exited and asked, "Boarding?"

"We want to trade them for some fresh horses; we'll pay any difference," Grant said.

"Yes, sir, when I inspect the horses, I'll let you know the price," the man said, taking the reins of Grant's horse from him, and continued, "When will you be needing the fresh horses?"

"Tomorrow morning," Grant said.

"Yes!" August said, clenching and pumping his fist.

"No boozing it up. We're getting up before dawn and heading out. We have a hard day's ride tomorrow, similar to today."

Dismounting from her horse, Abigail asked, "Why are we pushing harder?"

"On account that the old man is on the verge of death," August joked, walking his horse to the livery worker.

"He's fine," Abigail barked, defending Grant.

Grant overheard the conversation but chose to ignore it. He gathered his belongings and slung them over his shoulder. "We'll get rooms at the hotel right there," he said, pointing down the street.

"I don't have the money for that," August complained as he unbuckled his saddlebag.

"I'm paying for everyone. Just be here at the livery by four, we'll set out then; and again, don't stay up late, and no trouble," Grant said, giving August a hard stare before walking off.

August snickered and walked over to Abigail. "How about you and I go get a drink?"

"I'm taking a bath then going to bed."

"Oh, c'mon, live a little," he ribbed.

"August, I'm here to do something important, not have fun," she said in a chastising tone.

"Can't we do both?" he said, walking next to her towards the hotel. "Just one drink and I'll pay."

"I didn't think you had money?" she asked.

"So you'll come, then?" he asked.

They walked into the brightly lit lobby of the hotel. She grunted and said, "One drink but at the bar down here." She pointed to a small room off the lobby; against the wall was a short bar. A lone bartender stood cleaning a glass. Three tables were half full with men gambling.

August looked and frowned, it wasn't what he had in mind, but he'd take it. "Fine. When?"

"Ten minutes. I'll have one drink; then I'm taking a bath and going to bed," she said.

"Deal," he said with a broad smile.

***

Abigail heard August before even entering the hotel bar. By the sound of it, he'd already gotten himself into a little bit of trouble in the ten or so minutes it had taken her to check in and get settled.

"I don't care what you said, I ordered the cheap stuff," August barked at the bartender, who stood glaring at him.

Abigail sighed and marched into the room to help offset what could easily turn into a bad situation. "Excuse me, what's going on?" she asked, stepping up to the bar.

"Is this your husband?" the bartender asked.

August smiled and opened his mouth to say something inappropriate but was silenced by Abigail's raised hand.

"No, he's not, he's an associate, but if there's a misunderstanding, I might be able to help," Abigail said.

"Your associate here ordered the top-shelf whiskey, I gave it to him, he drank it, and when I asked for payment, he said he had ordered the standard pour, a lesser whiskey."

"I ordered your regular whiskey, you deaf bastard. Do I look like I can pay for your best?" August asked, stepping back from the bar and motioning with his hands at his worn clothing.

"I don't make judgments based on attire. I trust my patrons know what they can or cannot afford," the bartender exclaimed.

"So now you're calling me a liar?" August asked, pulling his right hand back near his pistol grip.

"Mister, I don't want any trouble," the bartender said, lowering his hands out of sight.

Abigail could see this going horribly wrong fast. "I'll pay for his whiskey, and pour one more for my associate."

"You sure?" the bartender asked.

"I'm sure," she replied to the bartender. Turning to face August, she said, "We don't want any trouble, do we?"

August grinned, swept his long dirty blond bangs to the side, and said, "You heard the woman; pour me another."

The bartender grunted under his breath and reached back, pulled the finer whiskey, and filled August's glass. "And for you, ma'am?"

"Root beer if you have it," she said.

"I have sarsaparilla. Will that be okay?"

"That'll be fine." She nodded.

The bartender stepped away from the bar, giving Abigail time to reprimand August.

"What the hell are you doing?"

"Looks like I was being taken advantage of until you came around and sorted it out," he replied sarcastically.

"You heard Grant, no trouble," she growled.

"I told you when I met you, or at least I thought I told ya, but just in case I didn't; I don't listen very well. I especially don't take orders from old farts like your pal Grant," August said.

"Grant is a good man," she protested.

"I wouldn't be so sure about calling him a good man," he snorted.

"You don't know him like I do," she said.

August sighed and slammed his drink with one gulp.

The bartender returned with a small brown bottle. He popped the cap and poured the dark brown carbonated drink in a mug. He slid it over and said, "Here you go, ma'am."

"One more," August barked at the bartender.

The bartender looked at Abigail.

"Don't look at her. I'm ordering," August growled.

"Yeah, but she's paying," the bartender countered.

"No, nope, I'll pay for this one," August said.

"Pay first; then I'll pour," the bartender said, holding the whiskey bottle close to his chest.

August resisted, like he had just told Abigail, he hated being told what to do. Resistance to anything remotely controlling was in his instincts.

The two men stood staring at each other in a sort of standoff.

"Fine!" August exclaimed, giving in. He dug into his pocket, pulled out a coin, and slammed it on the bar.

Seeing the coin, the bartender reached out and poured August's glass full. Not trusting August, he quickly took the coin and gave August the change.

August grabbed his glass, held it high, and "Here's to you, Miss Abigail."

Abigail tapped her glass against his and said, "You may not like to listen, but you're here on my job. You do what I say or what Grant says."

"Don't be such a stickler," he said.

The two chatted for a few minutes, talking mainly about the trip so far, when unexpectedly, a large man approached August. The man was drunk and looked clearly annoyed by August's earlier behavior. "Just who do you think you are, huh?"

August leaned back and laughed. "And who the hell are you?"

"The name is Cal, and I'm a local and frequent this little bar. I heard the trouble you were givin' Sam."

"Who's Sam?" August asked.

"The bartender, he's a friend of mine," Cal barked,

his hand drifting back to his pistol grip.

Abigail chirped up, "Listen, Cal, there's no trouble anymore. Let's talk about this, okay?"

"How about you keep your pretty mouth shut," Cal snapped, his hand now firmly touching the pistol grip.

Commotion suddenly broke out behind Abigail and August. It was Grant, and he had just hit another man over the head with the butt of his pistol. He took two steps towards Cal, reared back, and pistol-whipped him.

Cal fell to the floor unconscious.

Grant cocked the pistol and leveled it at Sam, who was now reaching underneath the bar. "Don't do it...please."

Startled by Grant's deliberate and decisive action, he lifted his arms up and groveled, "I said I didn't want trouble."

"Then you'll step away from that shotgun you have underneath the bar and keep your hands held high," Grant said, his pistol still pointed at Sam.

Sam did exactly as Grant ordered, and slowly walked away, keeping his hands held high.

"Good and, the rest of you, don't think about trying anything; I'll put a bullet in you faster than you can blink an eye," Grant threatened as he pointed his pistol at each person seated in the room.

"Holy cow!" August exclaimed, his eyes wide with joy.

"Go get your belongings. It's time to leave," Grant ordered.

"But we—" Abigail said, hoping to talk Grant out of

leaving.

"It's time to go, now," Grant snapped in anger.

August and Abigail fled the bar and raced to their rooms.

Grant backed out of the bar, ensuring he kept a watchful eye on everyone, especially the men he had knocked out. He picked up his saddlebags, slung them over his shoulder, and headed out of the hotel.

***

August and Abigail ran to the livery to find Grant had gotten fresh horses and had them saddled already.

"I take back the old-man talk," August said, tossing his saddlebags on the back of his new horse.

Grant walked over and slapped August upside the head. "I said no trouble. Don't you understand what that means?"

"Hey, I was just having a bit of fun is all," August said, rubbing where Grant had slapped him.

"If the hotel clerk hadn't come and gotten me, you'd both be dead," Grant said.

"So that's how you knew?" Abigail asked, voicing her thoughts out loud.

"Yes, that's how I knew, and the second I came down, I spotted you chitchatting with a man who was ready to kill you."

"I could have talked—" Abigail countered.

"You were talking yourself into an early grave. That man was only talking until his friend got in place. You were about to get ambushed."

"Sorry," Abigail said.

Something hanging on the door caught Grant's attention. He walked over and saw it was the wanted poster. He ripped it off and stuffed it in his pocket. He turned towards Abigail and said, "I don't want you to apologize, I want you to be ready. You need to know the difference between a man who is set to kill you and one who is all talk. That man and his partner were aiming to kill you both." He slowly mounted his horse.

"I'm really sorry. That won't happen again," Abigail said, a tone of shame in her voice.

"I'm pissed, I'm tired, and now we need to ride out of town instead of getting a nice rest," Grant growled.

August trotted up next to Grant and said, "You should have shot them."

"And that would have only made things worse. C'mon, you two, let's ride," Grant said, kicking his horse hard.

The horse reared up gently.

"Ya," Grant hollered just as his horse galloped out of town, with Abigail and August fast behind him.

CHAPTER TWELVE

TWENTY-TWO MILES NORTHEAST OF BILLINGS, MONTANA TERRITORY

SEPTEMBER 7, 1888

Grant slowed his horse to a canter as his coughing fit grew in intensity. He hadn't had one for over a day and knew one was coming sooner rather than later.

The sun hadn't risen yet to welcome the new day, but its presence was making itself known to the east. All were exhausted, as they'd been riding nonstop since fleeing Billings.

"Let's take a break," Abigail said, coming to a stop.

"I could use a piss," August said. He glanced at Grant and said, "I think the old man isn't doing too well."

Abigail trotted over to Grant, who was now stopped but sitting in his saddle, coughing loudly. "Can I help?"

He shook his head vigorously.

"I think we should take a break," she said.

He nodded.

She dismounted and looked around. It was light enough to see the lay of the land, the gentle roll of the hills accompanied by the rich smell of wild grasses.

"Do we have any food?" August asked, digging through his saddlebag.

"I have some hardtack and dried fruit," she said.

Grant got his coughing under control. He could feel

the warm blood on his hand. He gave it a glance and was shocked by how much there was. Disturbed by the sight, he quickly wiped it off on a handkerchief and dismounted. "Good call. Let's take a quick nap."

"Are you doing alright?" August asked.

"I'm fine. Got a bad cold is all; been in the lungs for a couple of weeks," he lied. He removed his bedroll and tossed it on the ground.

The three joined him. They neglected to make a fire. All they needed was a few hours of solid sleep; then they could keep riding.

Lying there looking up as the dark sky slowly turned blue, Abigail asked Grant, "Why didn't you shoot them?"

"Because doing so would have only made things worse," he replied.

"Is it because of your promise to your wife?" she asked.

"No, it's because killing them would have added to our problems."

"Have you lost your nerve, old man?" August prodded.

"I was prepared to shoot that bartender if he went for his shotgun. Does that make you feel better?" he asked.

"I still think you should have shot those guys. If they're as mean and bad as you said, they're better off dead," August said.

"You did say they were meaning to kill me and August," Abigail said, siding with August.

"Say I shot them. Right now we'd have a posse after

us, we wouldn't be able to rest, they would have ridden us down, and then what?"

"We shoot them too," August replied.

"There are times you shoot and times you don't; those men meant you harm, but mainly because August here came into their town and was causing trouble. Those two men found your actions reprehensible, and if you add liquor, they came to the conclusion that you should get shot for it. But back to why I didn't shoot, shooting them could have caused other men in the bar to turn on us. Just pistol-whipping isn't enough for some to start gunning for ya. I made a tactical decision based upon experience. And the reason we had to leave was that soon enough they'd awaken, and we'd have been in a gunfight," Grant explained.

"So we ran like cowards?" August grumbled.

"It's not running, it's advancing in the opposite direction," Grant replied.

"I call it staying alive," Abigail said, taking a mental note of everything Grant was saying.

"You don't run from a fight," August said.

"The fight was over, August. You're just being stupid," Abigail barked, growing tired of August's insubordination.

"Enough, let's all get some sleep," Grant said.

"Thank you," Abigail said.

"For what?" Grant asked.

"For saving us," she replied.

"Saving us? I could have handled them," August snorted as he chewed on a piece of dried fruit.

"Ha, you didn't even see the second man," Abigail challenged August.

"I was focusing on the big bearded guy. It was your job to watch my back," August fired back.

"Shut up, both of you, I need to rest," Grant barked.

Abigail closed her eyes, and just before falling asleep, she once more said, "Thank you, Mr. Toomey."

NORTH OF BIG CIRCLE RANCH, MILES CITY, MONTANA TERRITORY

Edward kicked Jed's cot and hollered, "Get your ass up."

"I'm getting up!" Jed said, his voice muffled by the pillow.

"It's seven, and we need to lay two miles of fence today on account you lay in bed sick with the liquor flu," Edward said, again kicking the cot.

"I'm getting up, you son of a bitch!" Jed yelled, jumping to his feet and getting inches from Edward's face. "I'm the boss's son; you'll treat me with respect."

"You're a piece of garbage, Jed. You're all talk. Even your father thinks you're a piece of garbage," Edward snapped.

Jed clenched his fists but remained silent.

Annoyed and out of patience, Edward threw open the cabin door and exited without closing it.

The bright light from the morning sun washed over Jed and chased the shadows from the dusty one-room cabin. Purgatory was small, no bigger than twelve feet by twelve feet, with a small outhouse located off the back.

Angry, he got his clothes on. He slipped on trousers over his long underwear and held them up with an old tattered pair of suspenders. He shoved his sore feet into his boots and got to his feet. Seeing a half-empty bottle of whiskey on the table, he went and took it in his grasp. As he went to put it to his lips, Edward stuck his head back in the cabin.

"Damn it, Jed. We need to go. I don't want to be out here longer than I have to. The sooner we get this fence up, the sooner we can head back to the ranch," Edward said. When he saw Jed drinking the whiskey, he stormed in and snatched the bottle from him. "No more. We need to work, now c'mon."

"To hell with you, Ed. I thought you were my friend," Jed yelled.

Edward slammed the bottle on the table and replied, "I was your friend until you got me into all sorts of trouble. You had to go and murder that Indian woman. I told you not to do that. I told you to leave that woman alone."

"She had it coming, you know she did," Jed whined.

"No, she didn't. She was minding her own business, and you got it in your head to go antagonize her."

"I didn't see you complaining then," Jed said.

"I did," Edward countered.

"You know, Ed, you can go screw yourself. Go ahead, go back out there and dig holes and string wire; it's all you're good for."

"It may be, but it's more than you're good for," Edward said, turning around and walking out.

Just before he exited, Jed picked up the bottle and threw it at Edward, striking the back of his head.

"Argh," Edward cried out in pain. He put his hand to the spot where he'd been hit and brought it back to see blood on his hand. "You busted my head open."

"I'll do more than that," Jed said and charged at him.

Unprepared for the assault, Edward didn't get his arms up before being tackled to the ground.

The two men wrestled and exchanged a few punches, with one of Edward's striking Jed in the temple. The blow was enough to daze Jed, who fell to the side. He shook his head to clear it, but Edward was unrelenting; he straddled Jed and delivered a heavy punch across Jed's jaw. Jed cried out. Edward came down again with another devastating blow, this time striking Jed in the nose and breaking it. "Ouch!" Jed cried out.

"Relent!" Edward said, his fist raised high, cocked and ready to punch again.

"Go to hell!" Jed shouted, spitting blood as he spoke.

Edward slammed his fist into Jed's face again. He recoiled and was ready to strike when he again said, "Relent."

"Okay, okay, I relent," Jed said.

Not sure, Edward kept his fist clenched and hovering over Jed's face. "I don't trust you."

"I'm telling the truth. I relent," Jed pleaded.

Sensing Jed had had enough, he lowered his arm and patted Jed on the chest. "Damn it, Jed, why are we doing this?"

"I don't know," Jed replied.

Edward shifted to get off Jed when he felt a searing pain in his back. He looked to his side and saw Jed had stabbed him. "What?"

Jed's face contorted into a sinister sneer. He pulled the bloody knife from Edward's body and quickly jabbed it in again.

Edward went to get off, but Jed grabbed and held him with his right hand. With his right, he stabbed him half a dozen more times, then took the blade and jammed it into the bottom of Edward's jaw and up into his skull. "You're right, you shouldn't trust me."

Edward gagged and coughed on blood. His eyes rolled back into his head, and he toppled over on the floor, his face hitting with a smack.

Jed looked at his old friend, his eyes still open. "I told you to leave me alone. It's all you had to do, just leave me alone, but no, you had to order me around. This is your fault." He scurried out from underneath the dead weight of Edward and got to his knees. He watched as the blood pooled around Edward. He was mesmerized by the sight of it, the dark thick red, the smell of it—it took him back to that day he'd killed Martha; there was a lot of blood then too. How would he explain this? he thought. It wasn't a matter of telling him what really happened, no, he'd have to dispose of Edward's body and say that he just ran off. Yes, that was what he'd do. With a sense of purpose for the day, Jed got to his feet and planned the specifics.

TWENTY-TWO MILES NORTHEAST OF BILLINGS, MONTANA TERRITORY

The three woke, but for Grant it was getting harder and harder. His body was sore, and the fatigue he was feeling was becoming unbearable. He'd slept a good five hours, but it felt like he hadn't slept a wink. A pain in his chest had made itself known, making him wonder how soon before he'd be unable to ride. He needed this bounty more than ever. He had committed to this job, and he needed to see it through. Yet he couldn't escape the nagging feeling that his body was beginning to fail him. Looking over at Abigail, he saw a strong, youthful and vibrant young woman. Billy had taught her well, and for that he was proud of his old friend. She had proven to be a very capable companion, but it was their other partner he had misgivings about. There was something about August he couldn't put a finger on, but it nagged him. He was going to have to keep a watchful eye on him.

"Hey, Abigail, come here," Grant said.

She promptly stepped over and said, "Yes, Mr. Toomey."

Grant pulled out the pocket watch he'd just received from Billy and said, "I want you to have this."

"Oh, no, I can't take that," she said, motioning with her hands.

"He won it fair and square, and it makes sense that you have it. I lost it years ago, and it should go to his heir or family, and that's you," Grant said, shoving the watch at her.

"Are you sure?"

"I'm positive; it's yours," he said.

She took the watch into her small hands and rubbed her right thumb over it. Holding and looking at the watch catapulted her to better times with her uncle Billy. She smiled and said, "Thank you, Mr. Toomey."

"You're welcome. You know, your uncle Billy would be proud of the woman I'm standing in front of."

"I hope he would."

"He would. I hope my Margaret grows to be a woman of strength and conviction like you," Grant said.

"I have no doubt she will. From my brief time with her, I found her to be not only sweet, but tenacious."

"That she is." He smiled.

Unable to control herself, she hugged Grant and said, "Thank you...for everything."

Shocked by the embrace, he replied, "You're very welcome."

She let go of him and ran back to her horse.

August watched the entire interaction and sneered at Grant. "What are you looking at? Saddle up. Let's ride."

CHAPTER THIRTEEN

FOUR MILES WEST OF MILES CITY, MONTANA TERRITORY

SEPTEMBER 8, 1888

Since leaving Billings two days before, they had covered one hundred and forty miles. It was a staggering distance for them to travel and had proven to be too much for Grant. His coughing had increased, and the fatigue from the lung disease compounded by the extreme distances made him unable to stay in the saddle. He passed out and toppled off his horse.

"Mr. Toomey!" Abigail cried out. She jumped from her horse and ran to his side. "Mr. Toomey, are you okay?"

Grant was lethargic and semi-responsive. He mumbled something unintelligible.

She unbuttoned his shirt and began to fan him.

"What's wrong with the old man?" August asked.

"He's not well," Abigail replied.

"I told you that days ago," August quipped.

"Shut up and get me some water," Abigail barked. She held Grant, and it appeared to her that he was beyond just exhaustion, it appeared that he was nearing death. His skin was pale, clammy and almost translucent and his eyes were barely open. Dried blood was caked on his lips and stubbled chin, with stains on his shirt.

August handed her a canteen and said, "I told you he was dying."

"Leave him be. He's just exhausted is all. We've ridden far, farther and faster than most can handle."

"The old man was right that we needed to ride hard. We can't wait for someone else to get that bounty; in fact, us sitting here with a full day ahead of us is foolhardy," August complained, looking towards the sun riding high in the sky.

"Abigail," Grant said just above a whisper.

She came to his side and knelt. Taking his hand, she said, "Yes."

"Where are we?" he asked.

"Just a few miles or so outside Miles City," she answered.

His eyes widened and he stirred. "We're almost there, and what time is it? It looks midday. No, we should complete the ride; get me up."

"No, lie down. You're not going anywhere," she said, pushing him back down onto his bedroll.

Weak and unable to resist, he let his body relax. "Can we talk...in private?" he asked, his gaze fixed on August pacing in the background.

"Do you mind going and giving the horses some food?" Abigail asked, looking over her shoulder at August.

"Why? I'm not allowed to hear what he has to say?" August asked, annoyed.

"That's exactly why," Abigail said.

August sneered and walked off.

"Abby, I'm not going to make it," Grant said.

"You are. You just need to rest," Abigail said.

"No, I can barely sit up. I don't think I can," Grant said.

"Stop saying that. We will rest here for the day and head in tomorrow," she said.

"I need just a few hours. Promise me you'll wake me in a few hours," he said, his eyes closing as the fatigue overtook him.

"You rest," she said softly as she wiped his face with a wet cloth. After he fell asleep, she sat back and pondered what she'd do if he died. Should she go on? Should she take his body back to his kids? What about the bounty? So many questions and not an answer for one. She was so close now, the thought of turning back only frustrated her. No, she'd have to press forward. She'd told him back in Rockland that she'd go ahead without him if he hadn't agreed, so therefore, she'd have to do the same now. But what if he died? again she asked herself. She hated thinking it, but it was a real situation to consider now. She had seen him deteriorate with each mile, growing weaker and weaker as they drew closer and closer to Miles City. Sadness welled up inside her when she thought of how his children would react to knowing he was dead. He wasn't like her father, he was a good man, a great father and provider. He was also very different than the man Uncle Billy had described. Minus the scene in Billings, he had been nothing but a gentleman, gracious, nice, sharing; yes, he was stern and assertive, but he wasn't the gunslinging killer that she had expected to see. No, lying on the ground next to her, taking shallow labored breaths, was a different man. Uncle Billy was right; it appeared his wife had changed him, turned him into something else.

August walked over to her and asked, "What should we do?"

"We wait, let him rest," she replied.

"For how long?"

"For as long as it takes," she answered.

"Right now there could be other bounty hunters converging, and we're here waiting on a dying man. Just leave him—"

She jumped to her feet and growled, "We're not leaving him." She poked August's chest with her index finger.

"Hey, I don't mean leave him for good, I mean to just go into town. It's right there. You said it's only a few miles away; we're so close. Maybe we could find out where Jed is. Sitting here doesn't help. We should be doing something," August argued.

"No!" Abigail said.

"He's right," Grant said, his voice straining.

Abigail craned her head back and asked, "You're awake? You should be resting, please. I'm sorry that we woke you."

Grant turned his head and repeated what he said, "He's right."

"See, even he agrees with me," August said, standing tall.

Abigail knelt down and said, "We're not going to

leave you."

"Go, please. Ride into town, go to the bars, saloons, wherever people gather. Listen to conversations; try to find out what you can. Here's a poster I found in Billings. It says to collect the bounty here," Grant said, pointing at the bottom of the poster.

"The Law Office of Busey and Company," she read out loud.

"Yes, you'll collect it from there. It's a privately held bounty; he'll have it," Grant said. "Talk to him maybe, if you have time, see if he knows anything. And did you read above?"

She looked up and exclaimed, "Ten thousand!"

"What?" August yelped, racing over to peek at the poster. "Hot damn, it is true."

"Why didn't you tell us?" Abigail asked.

"I was gonna, just was looking for the right time. A bounty that high is getting attention. You need to go with August into town, now," Grant said.

"We'd be gone for a long time. What if something happens to you?" she asked.

"I'll be fine. You're right, I need to rest...a lot; and it doesn't make sense for you two to sit here and watch me sleep. Go, find out what you can, then return," Grant said.

"Abby, I couldn't have said it better. Let's ride into town and see what we can find out. When we return, he'll be up, and we can all then make a coordinated plan off the information we gather," August said.

Abigail felt conflicted. Leaving Grant lying in the

middle of nowhere, possibly dying, just felt wrong, cruel even; but making the most of the time and tracking down Jed was the reason they were even there. From a practical standpoint, it was the right thing to do. If Grant was going to die in his sleep, he'd do so whether they were there or not.

"Abby, we only have maybe six hours or so of daylight," August said.

"Go, please, but promise me you won't do anything foolish, and no going after Jed until I help formulate the plan...promise me," Grant said.

"I promise," Abigail said, giving her word and signaling she was going.

August remained noticeably silent.

"Answer him," Abigail barked at August.

"I promise," August relented.

"Good, now ride, go and, Abby, be safe," Grant said.

She took his hand and squeezed it. "I will."

NORTH OF BIG CIRCLE RANCH, MILES CITY, MONTANA TERRITORY

"What do you mean he ran off?" Tuck asked, his hands firmly planted on his hips.

"I woke and his cot was empty. I went outside and his horse was gone. I can only guess that he'd had enough of shit details and left," Jed lied.

"Well, that no-good son of a bitch, after all we...Boyd had done for him, to just take off," Tuck complained.

"I know, it's horrible. I thought I knew him so well too," Jed said. "Say, I won't be able to finish up here by myself, so how about I ride back with you and tell my father what happened. I think I've spent enough time in Purgatory, no pun intended."

"Ah, I'm not so sure about that," Tuck said, looking around the cabin, shocked by the filth.

"Why not? I can't complete this fencing by myself. I'll grab my things," Jed said and turned around to pack his bag.

"Jed, no."

Turning back to face Tuck, Jed exclaimed, "What are you not telling me?"

"Your father gave very specific instructions. On no account—none, he was specific—were you to return until that fencing is in place."

"He most certainly didn't mean if I was left alone?"

"He said no account, that's pretty absolute, and you know your father, he has a way with words," Tuck said.

"C'mon, Tuck, you can't leave me out here by myself. How am I going to finish this job?"

"I suggest you keep working. Now, I'll be sure to explain everything to your father. I'll detail to him your situation. I'll leave out the fact you're drinking; he did say no boozing it up," Tuck said, holding up two empty bottles.

"Those were Edward's," Jed lied.

"It'll just be a day, no more. I'll ride back and tell him, and if he agrees, I'll come right back to get ya, okay?" Tuck asked.

"This is stupid, you know that?" Jed whined.

"I understand your predicament, but I work for your father, and I follow his instructions to the letter," Tuck said.

"Promise you'll tell him the second you return," Jed begged.

"I will. Now come and help me unload the supplies," Tuck said, pointing to the wagon parked in front of the cabin.

***

The two men finished unloading two weeks' worth of food and water into the cabin.

Hot and thirsty, Tuck said, "Do you have a glass?"

"Sure," Jed said, getting him a tin cup.

Tuck filled the cup with water and drank it down. "Comes in and goes out." He laughed. "Now I gotta take a piss."

"Ahh, the outhouse, don't use that," Jed warned, stopping Tuck from going around back.

"I wasn't going to use it. I was just going to take a leak out front. But what's wrong with the outhouse?" Tuck asked, stepping around Jed and unbuttoning his trousers.

"It's full. I need to dig another one," Jed said.

"Full? You boys must have taken a lot of dumps." Tuck laughed.

Jed looked next to the front door and saw a pickax; the thought of picking it up and hitting Tuck with it came to mind. If Tuck had gone to the outhouse, he'd no doubt have found where Jed had dumped Edward's body. "Yeah, it was almost full when we got here. He and I had been actually talking about digging a fresh one."

"Sucks for you, and glad I don't have to take a dump," Tuck said, buttoning his trousers and turning to see Jed standing only a few feet from him. "You okay?"

"Yeah, fine, ah, why do you ask?"

"On account of you standing right behind me as I pissed," Tuck said, giving Jed a wary eye.

"Oh, nothing, I just—hey, listen, please don't forget to tell my father the second you return," Jed said, shifting the conversation back to leaving the cabin.

"Damn it, Jed, I told you I would say something. Now, let me get out of here," Tuck said, climbing onto the wagon. He looked south and said, "It's only a two-hour ride, but damn, it feels like it takes twice as long."

"You're more than welcome to stay here," Jed said.

"No, thanks," Tuck said then sighed. "Listen, I feel bad for you, I do. I'll tell you what I'll do. No matter what, I'll come back out tomorrow, and if I come bearing bad news, I'll at least bring something that'll make your time out here…manageable."

"Whiskey?" Jed asked happily.

"I thought those were Edward's bottles?" Tuck joked.

"They were, but I don't mind tipping it back now and then," Jed said.

"Then I'll bring back a case of whiskey, okay?" Tuck asked.

"Thank you, you're a good friend," Jed said.

"I'll see you tomorrow," Tuck said and urged his horse onward.

MILES CITY, MONTANA TERRITORY

Abigail and August rode hard to town; timing was everything.

Being she was familiar with the town after having just been there a couple of weeks ago, her thought was to visit the very spot she and Uncle Billy had unfortunately gotten involved in the first place...the Elk's Head Saloon.

Arriving, they found the saloon relatively quiet. Inside, only a handful of people were gathered, several at a table playing poker and an equal number at the bar.

She looked and recognized the bartender; it was the same man. She prayed her weathered and dirty look would camouflage her enough, 'cause if he recognized her, that would be bad.

August bellied up to the bar and called out, "Bartender, two whiskeys. Oh, wait, you want..."

"Whiskey," she said, making her voice sound deeper.

August gave her an odd look then realized she was trying to disguise herself. "Sorry, two whiskeys."

The bartender grabbed a bottle and filled two shot glasses. "You two passing through?"

"Yeah, on our way to Billings to work in our uncle's hardware store," August replied, hastily making up a story.

The swinging doors of the saloon swung open, and

in came Tuck. He marched up next to August and leaned in. "Hey, Bob, how ya doing?"

"Good, Tuck," Bob said, pouring a glass of whiskey for Tuck.

Tuck took the glass and tossed it back. "Another."

"What's new?" Bob asked.

"Nothing, just returned from dropping off supplies to the boss's boy up at Purgatory. Say, have you seen Edward?"

"Edward? The tall lanky one who runs with Jed?" Bob asked.

"Yeah, him," Tuck asked.

Overhearing Jed's name mentioned, Abigail leaned closer to August, who was actually standing next to Tuck and listening intently as well.

"Nope, haven't seen him since Boyd clamped down on anyone coming into town," Bob said. "That leads me to this question, when will Mr. Wallace let everyone come back? It's hurting my business."

"If your business is hurting, bring it up with him. He might help you out," Tuck said, slamming his drink and pushing the glass towards Bob. "Fill it up."

"I get some business, but it's not enough. I'm hurting without everyone from the Big Circle Ranch," Bob complained.

"Stop bitching to me. Take it up with Boyd. Oh, I need a case of whiskey, your cheapest stuff."

"Thirsty, are we?" Bob said, walking towards the back.

"No, I'm taking it out to Jed tomorrow. Poor bastard

is stuck out there all alone." Tuck laughed.

Bob laughed too then disappeared into the storeroom.

Tuck took his glass, turned around, and faced out towards the room to get a good look at everyone in the place. He scanned the room carefully, looking for anyone from the ranch. When he got to August, he said, "Hey, friend, who are you?"

"Just passing through," August said with a smile, keeping his head low.

"And you next to him, are you passing through too?" Tuck asked Abigail.

Abigail nodded. She kept her head faced away from Tuck and her head down.

"You wouldn't happen to be bounty hunters, would you?" Tuck asked.

"No, sir, just prospectors on our way to Idaho," August replied, mixing up his stories.

Tuck leaned down to get a better look at August's face and asked, "Prospectors, huh?"

"Yes, sir."

"Hmm."

Bob returned, and in his arms he cradled a crate of whiskey. He placed it on the bar and asked, "Add it to your tab?"

"Yeah," Tuck said, turning back around. He put his glass down, picked up the crate, then turned back to August. "Happy prospecting in Idaho."

"Prospecting in Idaho? I thought you told me you were going to work for your uncle's hardware store in

Billings?" Bob asked.

"Shit!" August grumbled under his breath.

Abigail felt the hairs on her back rise; she knew this was about to go sideways. She placed her hand on the back strap of her pistol and gripped it.

Tuck stopped, turned and asked, "Which is it, boy?"

August stood tall, turned to face Tuck, who was still holding the crate, and said, "You know something, I'm not heading to Billings or Idaho, I'm headed to Purgatory." He pulled his Colt, cocked it and fired. His first shot struck Tuck in the shoulder.

Tuck dropped the crate and stumbled backwards.

Abigail drew. She saw Bob reaching behind the bar. Not waiting to give him a verbal warning, she cocked her Colt and squeezed the trigger. Her aim was true, with her shot striking Bob squarely in the chest.

Bob fell back against the back bar, smashed into glasses and bottles, and dropped to the floor.

She cocked the pistol again, spun around, and waited to engage anyone else in the bar, but no one moved.

August faced the bar and hollered, "Don't any of you bastards try a thing!"

With both Abigail and August focused on the others in the bar, they missed Tuck crawling towards the back door. When the door creaked open, August looked but only saw a glimpse of Tuck running out.

"He's alive!" August cried out and went to race after Tuck, but Abigail grabbed him by the arm.

"We don't have time," she said.

"He'll alert the others," he exclaimed.

"It's too late. We need to go get Grant and go after Jed now," she said. She walked up to the oldest man she saw in the place, pointed the pistol at his face, and asked, "Where's Purgatory?"

"I...I...um, I don't know where that is," the old man stuttered.

"Who here knows where Purgatory is? Tell me or the old man gets it," she threatened. As she waited for an answer, she prayed someone would tell her so she didn't have to shoot the old man.

A voice from the back of the saloon called out, "It's north of the Big Circle Ranch. It's an old hunting cabin."

Abigail walked to the back and saw a middle-aged man sitting by himself. She hadn't seen him when they entered the saloon. "Draw me a map," she said, tossing a notepad and pencil in front of him.

"Why, you're a woman," the man said, astonished when he saw she was female.

"Aren't you the observant one? Now shut up and draw me a map," she said, pointing at the notepad with her pistol.

The man nervously took the pencil and sketched out a detailed map of where the cabin could be found and handed it back to her.

"How long will it take for him to get to the ranch?" she asked.

"An hour," he replied.

"How far is the ranch from Purgatory?"

"Oh, I'd say two hours, maybe less," he answered, his voice cracking a bit.

She uncocked her Colt, holstered it and said, "Thank you." She spun around and cried out, "Time to go."

August followed her out, taunting the patrons as he went.

Outside, she said, "We have maybe four hours. We can do it, but we don't have time to mess around."

"I'll go to Purgatory. I'll meet you there," August offered.

"No, we ride together; we're a team," she said, mounting her horse.

"Fine," he said, climbing on his horse.

"Let's go get Mr. Toomey," she said, then raced away with August close behind her.

FOUR MILES WEST OF MILES CITY, MONTANA TERRITORY

Abigail rode as fast as she could, almost falling twice from her horse. Never in her life had she ridden with such fury. Her pace was so fast that August was finding it difficult to keep up.

She arrived at the campsite well ahead of August, to find Grant sleeping. "Mr. Toomey, wake up."

Grant opened his eyes and asked, "Am I dead?"

"Not yet, but we know where he is," she exclaimed.

"Good."

"But there's no time to waste. We need to get to Purgatory fast," she said.

He sat up and asked, "What's happened?"

"It wasn't our fault. I didn't mean to shoot the man,

but he was pulling a gun, and you said you need to know if a man's aiming to kill you, and this man was, so I shot him," she rattled off.

"You shot someone?" he asked, sitting up further.

"Yes, the bartender, he was pulling a gun. I had to, please believe me," she said.

"I believe you. It's fine," Grant said, looking around. "Where's August?"

"He's coming, he's just slow," she said.

"Where's Jed?"

"He's here," she said, taking out her notebook and opening it to the page with the map. "He's right there, that X. It's a cabin called Purgatory. Don't ask me why they call it that, but he's there alone."

"How do you know we need to get there fast? Will he be alerted?" Grant asked, taking a labored breath, his chest hurting.

"Yes, there was another man. I can't remember his name…oh yeah, Tuck, that's it, he works for Mr. Wallace, Jed's father. He was there and August shot him, but he didn't kill him. He managed to escape. I'm sure he's going to warn Jed."

"What do we know about this Purgatory? Is it a house? Are there outbuildings?" Grant asked, now getting to his feet.

"It's an old hunting cabin? I don't know about outbuildings."

"Saddle my horse, hurry," he ordered.

She jumped up and did as he asked.

He pressed his eyes closed, took several deep and

painful breaths, opened his eyes, and said, "Abby, are you ready?"

"I'm ready, Mr. Toomey."

"Good, 'cause we're about to secure your first bounty," Grant said, walking over to his horse. He placed his left foot in the stirrup and, using all his strength, pulled himself up and straddled the horse. He gave Abigail a glance and winked. "Let's ride."

The two sprinted away. Over a slight rise, August was coming at them. They passed him going at a full gallop.

August steered his horse around and cried out, "Wait for me!"

BIG CIRCLE RANCH, MILES CITY, MONTANA TERRITORY

Tuck arrived at the ranch to find most of the men out working. He rode to the main house, got off his horse, his arm dangling due to the wound in his shoulder, and cried out, "Mr. Wallace! Mr. Wallace!"

Several people, including Clement, came out. "What the hell?"

"Bounty hunters, they know where Jed is," Tuck said.

"How many?" Clement asked.

"Two," Tuck said. "They killed Bob and shot me."

"Go get bandaged up," Clement said.

Boyd threw open a side door. "Clement, what in tarnation is going on?"

"Boss, there's bounty hunters headed to Purgatory," Clement said.

Boyd's eyes widened. He stared hard at Clement and said, "Gather what men you can. Meet me at the stables. You, go to the armory; bring down a wagon of rifles and sidearms. Hurry!"

Each man ran off, except for Tuck, who stood holding his shoulder.

"How did you get shot?" Boyd asked.

"They ambushed me," Tuck answered.

"Where?"

"The Elk's Head."

Boyd's nostrils flared. "Weren't you supposed to be delivering supplies to Jed?"

"I did, sir, I did it before. I was coming back and made a round to check and see if Bob had come across any new people, bounty hunters, in town. You asked me to do that now and then."

Boyd rubbed his chin, thought and said, "You're right. Go inside; see one of the housekeepers. Get your arm cleaned up; then meet us down at the stables."

"You want me to ride with you?" Tuck asked, surprised.

"Yes, I need every available man. You can ride, right?"

"Yes."

"Shoot?"

"I can manage, sir."

"Then hurry up and be down there as quick as you can," Boyd hollered. He looked to the sky and said,

"Lord, watch over my boy, but if this is his day, make it quick."

NORTH OF BIG CIRCLE RANCH, MILES CITY, MONTANA TERRITORY

Each hoof plant his horse made rattled Grant's body. He was using every single last ounce of strength he could muster to just stay in the saddle. He was so close, so very close to bagging Jed and giving his children a chance. All he needed to do was make it a little bit longer.

Abigail had ridden ahead of both men to scout, and as she came upon a rise, she spotted a long cabin in a shallow valley. She pulled back hard on her horse, causing it to come almost to a standstill. She turned back towards the oncoming men and waved.

"She's found it," August cried out, whipping his horse to go faster. "Come on, old man."

Unable to go faster, Grant stayed at his pace until he reached them.

"Down there, I think that's Purgatory," Abigail said, pointing.

Grant removed a small set of binoculars from his saddlebag and put them to his eyes. He adjusted and focused until the cabin came into view, although his hand's trembling was making it hard to see.

Seeing he was having trouble, Abigail reached over and said, "Let me."

Grant smiled and handed the binoculars to her. When she took them, he looked down and exhaled heavily. He wasn't sure how much help he was going to be, but he'd give it his all.

"I don't see anything, no movement. There's a single horse tied up out front, that's it," she said.

The cabin door opened, and out came Jed. He ran to the outhouse and went inside.

"Did he just go into the shitter?" August asked, able to make out what had happened with the naked eye.

"Yeah, he did. Mr. Toomey, should we ride in?" Abigail asked.

"The man in the bar said he was alone?" Grant asked.

"Yes," Abigail replied.

"This is stupid. He's alone and he's taking a dump. I'm going," August barked. He kicked the side of his horse and took off down the slope towards the cabin.

"August!" Abigail hollered.

"Go, hurry," Grant said.

Abigail tossed the binoculars to Grant, slapped her horse, and bolted away, losing her hat as she went. Like before, she pushed her horse hard and soon caught up with August. A few seconds later she was ahead of him, and seconds later was leading him at a good clip and moving away.

"Damn it, woman!" August spat.

Knowing he needed to be down there too, Grant sucked up the pain and fatigue and followed them down.

Jed exited the outhouse sooner than Abigail or August expected. He looked up and saw them coming. For a second he wondered who they could be as he squinted to get a clear view, then realized they must be bounty hunters. He sprinted to the cabin and dove inside.

Undeterred that the element of surprise had been blown, Abigail pressed ahead.

Jed grabbed a Winchester rifle, cycled the lever action, and went to a window. He saw the first rider, aimed, and just before pulling the trigger, he paused. He blinked to clear his vision and noticed the rider was a woman. His shock wore off when he saw the second rider not far behind. He put his attention back on Abigail, took aim, and squeezed. The rifle fired, but his aim was off.

Abigail heard the crack and whiz of the bullet fly by her. Her heart was racing, but she was so close she could taste it.

Jed cycled the lever action again, aimed, and once more fired, this time pulling the trigger. This shot was further off then the first. It impacted the dirt twenty feet behind Abigail.

Hearing the second shot only made Abigail ride harder. She was closing in, all she needed was ten seconds, and she knew how to get it. Holding the reins in her left hand, she pulled her Colt with her right, cocked it, aimed as best she could at the broken window Jed was shooting from, and squeezed. The pistol fired unexpectedly. Unlike Jed, her aim was true, even from horseback.

The bullet slammed through the top pane of the window and struck Jed in the top of his left shoulder. He cried out in pain, dropped his rifle, and cursed loudly.

Abigail cocked the Colt again and fired another round, this one mainly to provide her cover. She repeated this another time until she had arrived. She leapt from the horse, ran to the side of the cabin, and called out, "Jed, surrender. I can take you dead or alive."

"Do you swear you won't shoot me?" Jed cried out. He knew surrendering was a death sentence too, but it gave him time to plan an escape if possible.

"I won't shoot you. Now come on out," Abigail said.

August arrived, jumped from his horse, pistol in hand, and ran up alongside Abigail.

"I think I hit him," Abigail said.

"You did?" August asked, surprised to hear she'd accomplished that from the back of a horse at a full gallop.

"Jed, come on out," Abigail said.

"I need your partner to also agree not to shoot me," Jed said, blood running down his left arm.

Abigail nudged August.

"I won't shoot you, although you should be shot," August called out.

Annoyed as usual with August, she jabbed him with her elbow.

"Well, he should," August said.

"You're really going to collect because I killed some savage? Is this where the world is going?"

"Just come out. I don't have time to argue with you," Abigail said.

Grant arrived but didn't dismount. "Abby, what's going on?"

"He's inside. I shot him," she said.

Hearing the name, Jed thought for a second; then it came to him. "Is that you, Abigail Bartlett?"

"Jed, just get your ass out here, or we'll burn this cabin to the ground with you in it!" Grant yelled then dismounted his horse.

"There's another one of you?" Jed asked, peeking out the window to see Grant walking toward the cabin entrance. "Who are you?"

"Never mind that. We're here to take you in. Now I'd prefer to kill you, as it's easier and it pays the same, but having you come out alive can also be arranged," Grant said.

"I told them I'll come out. Just promise me you won't shoot me," Jed pleaded.

"We're not going to shoot you. Now come out," Grant said.

Unsure but with no recourse, he trusted they'd keep their word. "I'm coming out."

Abigail stepped away from the side of the cabin, pistol in hand, and readied herself.

Jed unlocked the door and slowly opened it. He snuck a quick look, then opened it fully. "I'm stepping out. Don't shoot. I'm unarmed." He emerged from the cabin, barefoot and in blood-soaked long underwear. His arms were raised above his head as he cautiously walked out.

Upon seeing him, thoughts of Uncle Billy and Aunt Nell being slain by him popped into Abigail's mind. Her anger swelled. She marched over to him and struck him in the head.

Jed dropped to his knees. He looked up at her and said, "You said you wouldn't shoot me."

"And I haven't...yet," she said, the pistol now pointed at his face with the hammer cocked back.

"It is you. Well, what do you know? Abby Bartlett. Girl, you look like you've grown up fast," Jed said.

"I had to," she said.

Grant wanted to stop her from what he felt was coming but also knew Abigail needed this to play out however it was going to for her own well-being.

August, on the other hand, stood with a large grin. He enjoyed the show of violence playing out in front of him.

"I want to let you know that what happened that night, that was my father. You know him, I have—heck, no one has a say. If he says it has to be done, it has to be done," Jed said weakly, defending the murder of Billy and Nell.

"You're a cold-blooded murderer, Jed Wallace, and I've ridden a thousand miles since then to arrive right here to kill you," Abigail said as she gently applied pressure to the trigger.

"You promised you wouldn't shoot me, you swore," he pleaded.

"Damn you to hell, Jed Wallace. This is for Martha Emery and Uncle Billy and Aunt Nell."

"No!" Jed cried out.

The Colt fired.

The bullet exploded from the short barrel and

slammed into the side of Jed's head, exiting the opposite side, splattering blood, brain and skull onto the ground. Jed's body folded over and fell to the ground.

A single swirl of smoke came from the barrel of her pistol. She lowered it, then placed it back in her holster. She took a step closer to Jed and looked down as his body involuntarily twitched.

"That was beautiful," August crowed with joy.

She had done it. After weeks on the trail, she had completed her first job, one that also gave her the revenge she had been seeking. She knew there wasn't much time to hover, as word had no doubt reached Boyd at the Big Circle Ranch, and soon a posse of sorts would converge on them.

Grant stepped up behind her, a trickle of blood on the side of his mouth.

Still looking at Jed's body, she asked, "You okay, Mr. Toomey?"

"Still standing," he replied. "Let's put his body on that horse and deliver him to the attorney in town."

"It feels odd," Abigail said, her gaze still upon Jed, his eyes still open.

"What feels odd?" Grant asked.

"I've killed three men now, my father, that bartender, and now him; this feels a bit different," she said, trying to explain.

"How?" Grant asked.

"Killing my father gave me relief, killing that bartender was justified, absolutely no emotion around that, but Jed—this, this felt good. Is there something wrong with me?"

"I'm not one to make such judgments; that's between you and your maker," Grant said.

"And you wouldn't have killed him?" she asked.

"I told you, my days of killing are over. This was yours to do or not do."

"Why didn't you stop me if you don't believe in killing anymore?" she asked.

"'Cause we have free will. This was your choice, not mine. Jed was an evil man; there's justification for killing a man like him. Heck, some don't even call him a man, some would call him an animal, and they wouldn't be wrong. The world is full of people, some are good and they do bad things, but the world is also full of just bad, evil people; he was one of them. The world is better with him gone. If you hadn't killed him, then the marshal would have."

Abigail heard the distinct cocking of a pistol and tore her gaze to see August stepping up behind Grant, his pistol pointed at Grant's back. "Whoa, what the hell are you doing?" Abigail asked.

In a frantic voice he blurted, "He's the son of a bitch that killed my parents!"

"What? What are you saying?" Abigail asked.

"Him, he's the man I went looking for in Rockland. He's Abraham Tillis, now known as Grant Toomey," August shouted.

"August, put the gun down," Abigail said.

"This has nothing to do with you, Abby. Don't get in the way. I'd hate to have to kill you too, but I will,"

August roared.

Grant slowly turned around with his hands up. "You got me, kid."

"I should blow you away right now, but I need to know," August spat.

"Know what?" Grant asked.

"Why? Huh? Why did you kill my parents? They were good people. Their death changed my life. I could have been a good person, but seeing their bodies lying there, my mother's eyes wide open, the look of terror on her face—I could never get those images out of my head," August cried out, his hand beginning to tremble.

Abigail sized up August and began to strategize how she'd end this standoff.

"It was an accident, plain and simple. Me and Billy were given the wrong house by a bad informant. When we came in that night, your father drew on me. I couldn't really see who it was because of the dim light, but I saw the muzzle pointed at me. I did what came naturally then, I shot him; then your mother came out, with a shotgun; again I acted on instinct and gunned her down. After discovering I'd killed the wrong people, I fled. I spent the next year in a drunken state until Latanne found me. She gave me new hope that I could move forward, and I did, but I never forgave myself for killing your parents."

"Why didn't you turn yourself in? Huh? You could have done that and faced justice, but you ran like a coward!" August hollered.

"You're right, I ran, and I am a coward," Grant admitted.

"I want you on your knees, now!" August screamed, sweat pouring off his brow and face.

"Don't do this," Abigail pleaded.

"When did you know?" Grant asked.

"The second I came up on you two at that campsite, but I hid my knowledge once you offered me a position on this job. You see, I need the money, so I figured I'd do the job, kill you, then take the money," he confessed. "Sorry, Abby, I'm taking Jed's body back into town. Take that rope there and tie it to that post."

"You're double-crossing me too?" Abigail asked, although not entirely shocked; she'd had a sense about him since Pocatello.

"It's nothing personal. I need the money," August said. "And you, get on your knees. I want you to beg forgiveness like a dog."

"I am sorry for what happened and how it changed your life. If you're aiming to kill me, just do it," Grant said, resigned to his fate.

"August, you're making a mistake," Abigail said.

"I said go tie that rope to the post," August said, pointing to a long rope on the ground near her.

"Kill me but don't double-cross Abby. She worked hard for this and deserves her cut of the share. You can take mine. Okay?" Grant offered.

"No!" August yelled at Grant. He looked at Abigail and yelled, "Pick up the damn rope!"

Seeing an opportunity, Abigail bent down, grabbed the rope, and tossed it at August, who was just a few feet away.

Not expecting her to do that, he flinched, giving Grant the chance to move on him.

Grant grabbed his arm and held it down. The two began to wrestle for the pistol when it suddenly went off.

Grant stumbled back and fell to the ground. He looked down and saw blood beginning to soak through his shirt.

August stepped forward, cocked the pistol, pointed it at Grant's head and said, "Go to—" But before he could finish his sentence, Abigail drew her pistol and shot August through the temple. August dropped to the ground dead.

She went to Grant's side and asked, "How bad is it?"

"Gut shot," he answered.

"Get up. I need to take you to a doctor," she said, pulling on him to rise.

Grant shook his head and said, "No time for that. We need to get Jed to the attorney; no time for a doctor."

"There's time, now c'mon," she said, pulling at him harder.

"No, there's not," he replied, pointing off in the distance.

Abigail looked and saw a dust cloud about three-quarters of a mile away. In the center of the cloud was a team of riders, no doubt from the Big Circle Ranch.

Grant struggled to his feet. With urgency he and Abigail picked up Jed and tossed him over August's horse. "Now go to that attorney and collect the bounty."

"You're coming with me," Abigail exclaimed.

"We'll never make it together. I'm going to cause a

diversion, which will allow you to get away."

"No!" she cried out.

Taking her hand in his, he said, "You being Billy's niece makes you like family to me. He'd protect my kin and I'm protecting his. Now go."

"I won't. We can fight them off," she said defiantly.

"Damn it, Abby," he said loudly. "I'm dying already, and now I'm gut shot. I don't have much longer. I only ask you take my share to my kids. Can you promise me you'll do that?"

Tears welled in her eyes, but she held off from fully crying. Realizing he was determined to stay and fight, she relented. "I will, I promise."

"Thank you. Now go, no time to waste. If you ride that way, you can hide your escape in the ravine. They won't even see you."

She mounted her horse, and with the reins of August's horse in her hand, she gave Grant one last look before racing off.

Grant watched her go for a few seconds before turning and going to his horse to grab his rifle. He pulled his Winchester from the scabbard and took up a position behind a boulder. "Alright, you sons of bitches, let's dance."

MILES CITY, MONTANA TERRITORY

Abigail raced into town at a full gallop, slowing only when she reached the attorney's storefront. She jumped from the horse, sprinted to the door, and tried to open it only to find it was locked. "Oh, c'mon." She peered inside and saw it was dark. Knowing her time was limited, she began to bang loudly. "Anyone here? Open up!"

The last time she'd seen Grant, he was engaging the large pack of riders, who numbered over a dozen. She had watched in amazement as he stuck to the promise he'd given his deceased wife, to kill no more. One by one, she'd watched him shoot the horses out from underneath the riders. However, she knew he'd never get them all before they were on top of him. There was no doubt it was Grant's last stand.

"Open up!" she yelled, banging on the front door.

A light appeared from the back of the office.

She watched a man emerge from the shadows, rubbing his eyes. He walked up to the locked door and peered out. He gave her a peculiar look then saw the body hanging from the horse. He furrowed his brow and asked, "Are you here for the bounty?"

"Yes, I need to collect it and fast," she said frantically.

He unlocked the door and opened it wide. "I need proof. Is that Jed Wallace?"

She grabbed him by the nape of his neck and dragged him outside. She went to Jed's body, lifted his head, and said, "This is Jed Wallace. Proof enough?"

He put on his spectacles and said, "Yep, that is him."

"The bounty, now!" she exclaimed.

"What's the rush?" he asked.

"Why do you think? Hurry up."

"It will take me a few minutes to open the safe

and…" he said, slowly walking back into his office.

Frustrated with his lethargic demeanor, she aimed to get him motivated. She drew her Colt, cocked it, and said, "Hurry up!"

Seeing the muzzle of the pistol, he cried out, "Okay, okay." He rushed to the back of his office and opened the safe. He removed a sack of coins and a sack full of notes. He stood and gave them to her. "Ten thousand as promised."

She opened the sacks and peeked inside. Having never seen ten thousand dollars, she didn't have anything to judge it by. "This is all of it?"

"Every cent," he confirmed.

"What are you going to do with Jed?" she asked.

"Give him to Boyd, I imagine. We normally would stage them on the street, but I don't think Boyd would take kindly to that," he said. "Who are you anyway?"

She tipped her hat and replied, "Name is Abby Sure Shot from Abilene, and it was nice doing business with ya." She ran out of the office, leapt onto her horse, and raced off, heading southwest towards Rockland, Idaho.

NORTHERN EDGE OF BIG CIRCLE RANCH, MILES CITY, MONTANA TERRITORY

Grant had managed to escape from the cabin ahead of Boyd's posse's arrival, but not before being hit a couple of times, once in the shoulder and once in the arm. His diversion had worked as he lured them in his direction. His wounds were beginning to slow him down, and soon they'd catch him. In the distance he saw a solitary peachleaf willow tree standing tall among the high grasses. It was the only feature that stuck out, and it looked to Grant like a fine place to die.

He had lost a considerable amount of blood from the numerous gunshots, but the one in his lower abdomen was causing him the most pain and blood loss. Unsure of how much longer he had, he pledged he'd stay alive just long enough to make it to the shade of the tree. He prodded his horse and hollered, "Go!"

His horse heeded his command and bolted at a full gallop across the gentle rolling hills, stopping only when he pulled on the reins just shy of the tree.

Grant grunted as he shifted in his saddle. He pulled his hand away from his stomach and was shocked by the volume of blood that had soaked through his shirt and down his trousers. He glanced up at the tree and smiled. "This will do." As he attempted to dismount, he lost his footing and toppled off the horse, hitting the hard ground beneath him with a thud. "Argh." He slowly got to his knees, reached for his rifle in the scabbard, and pulled it out. Not wanting the horse in the way, he smacked her hard on the rump and yelled, "Get! Go!"

The horse neighed loudly before sprinting off.

Grant crawled to the base of the trunk and sat down. He let out a heavy sigh and rested his head against the thick bark. His thoughts instantly went to Margaret and George. He wondered what sort of life they'd have. Would Margaret find the perfect man and settle down? Would she have the ten children she often said she wanted as a young girl, or would she be fine with only a couple? Was George going to be happy being a farmer, or would he pursue other ambitions? He trusted Abigail would bring them his share of the bounty, giving them a substantial sum to live off of after paying off the farm's debts.

A slight vertigo hit him. He pressed his eyes closed and let it pass. He was sure it was from the blood loss. When he reopened his eyes, he saw riders coming his way. He squinted and counted seven; his stand at the cabin had paid off.

He checked his weapons, which included his Winchester rifle and his Colt. After he loaded them, he placed them on his lap and looked up. The riders were closer, their silhouettes shimmering like an oasis in the distance from the bright mid-afternoon sun. He estimated they'd be on top of him within five minutes or less, and they'd no doubt come in shooting.

He lifted the rifle and took aim, but his arms were so weak and trembling that he couldn't keep the sights locked on a target to make it an effective shot.

"Grant, put down your arms and come with me," a gentle voice called out.

He lowered the rifle and looked around but saw no one. "Who is that?"

"Grant, my love, it's time. Put your guns down and join me," the voice said. This time it sounded louder and closer to him.

Disturbed, Grant cried out, "Who is that? Show yourself."

A blinding bright light to his left suddenly appeared.

He looked away for a second, then looked back and allowed his eyes to adjust. When they did, he saw his beloved wife, Latanne, standing above him. She was adorned in a long flowing white dress, and her skin was as white as porcelain.

"Latanne?" he cried out.

She approached and knelt next to him. "My love, it's time."

"But…" he said, pointing towards the riders coming.

She extended her slender arm and caressed his face. "Pay no mind to them. It is time to come with me."

He touched her hand and began to weep. "I've missed you for so long. There hasn't been a day since you left me that I haven't thought about you."

"I know," she said sweetly.

"How could you know that?" he asked, bewildered.

"Because I've been with you the entire time," she confessed.

"Wait, this is a dream, right? I'm passed out from blood loss. You're not real," he said.

"*Mon amour*, it is me, your French flower. I am real, and now you must come."

"The children, what will come of them?" Grant asked.

"They will be fine."

"How do you know that?" he asked, confused by her responses.

"I can see them, and as soon as you come with me, you will too," she said, taking his hand and lifting him to his feet.

Grant felt an odd sensation wash over him as all the pain in his body vanished. "The pain...it's gone."

She nodded and glanced just past him.

He looked back and saw his body still lying against the tree, his eyes open in a death stare. "That's me. I'm...dead."

"Only your body is dead, now come," she said and walked him towards the light.

CHAPTER FOURTEEN

BIG CIRCLE RANCH, MILES CITY, MONTANA TERRITORY

SEPTEMBER 9, 1888

Boyd leaned back in his thick leather chair and folded his arms upon hearing that Frederick Busey was just outside his office door. He'd come to deliver Jed's body but was told he couldn't leave until he met with Boyd.

"Let him in," Boyd ordered Tuck.

Frederick timidly walked in and stood a safe distance from Boyd's desk.

"I hear you just brought my son's body to the ranch," Boyd said, opening the top right desk drawer.

"Yes, sir." Frederick gulped.

Boyd pulled out a pistol and placed it on top of the desk. He leaned back in his seat and asked, "How did you come by his body?"

Seeing the pistol, Frederick grew tense. "Ahh, a woman, she brought him in yesterday morning, sir."

"A woman? Who? What was her name?" Boyd asked.

"Um, she said her name was Abby Sure Shot."

"Abby Sure Shot? What the hell kind of name is that?" Boyd laughed.

"That's what she told me."

"And did you pay her the bounty money?" Boyd

asked, glancing towards the pistol.

Fearful on how to respond, Frederick just remained quiet.

Breaking the pause, Boyd spoke louder. "Did you pay her the bounty?"

"Yes."

"How much?"

"Ten thousand, Mr. Emery's will and testament called for the bounty to be increased to ten thousand in the event of his untimely death."

"You paid this Abby Sure Shot ten thousand dollars?"

"Yes."

"Did you think to alert anyone from the ranch before you made this transaction?"

"Ahh, sorry, no."

"Did this Abby Sure Shot tell you where she was going or where she came from?" Boyd asked.

"She said Abilene."

"Abby Sure Shot from Abilene, seems like a made-up name if I ever heard one. So what you're telling me is you don't know who you gave that money to yesterday."

"Correct, but in my defense, the parameters of Mr. Emery's final wishes didn't reference getting a positive identification of the bounty hunters."

"Mr. Busey, can I trust you in the future not to just let people ride off with large sums of cash without telling me?"

"Yes, sir, from now on."

"Good, now go," Boyd said, waving Frederick away.

Not wanting to stay an extra second in Boyd's presence, Frederick nodded and raced off.

When the door closed, Boyd turned to Tuck and asked, "Ever heard of this person?"

"No, boss," Tuck said, his arm in a sling. "I didn't see a woman in the saloon yesterday."

"Well, find out what you can," Boyd said.

"I'll send some men to Abilene, sir," Tuck said and headed for the door.

"No, no, don't do that. Just ask around. Send a letter or telegram to our friends in the Abilene stockyards," Boyd said, stopping Tuck.

"Are you sure, sir?" Tuck asked.

"I'm positive. We need all of our men here working. We've already lost too much because of my damn fool son," Boyd said.

"Any idea who those two men were? The one at Purgatory and the body we found at the tree?" Boyd asked.

"The man at Purgatory was the man who shot me; the older man, never seen him before," Tuck said.

"He looked familiar," Boyd said, thinking.

"Want me to circulate a drawing of their faces?" Tuck asked.

"No need."

"I'll get to sending a telegram right away, then, to Abilene," Tuck said and exited the room.

Boyd crossed his arms and thought about the death of Jed. A tingle of sentiment sat in his heart, but if he were honest, he was glad his troubled son was gone.

"Clement!" Boyd cried out.

Walking into the room promptly, Clement approached the desk and said, "Yes, sir."

"Plan a funeral service for Jed. I want to have it tomorrow."

"Yes, sir."

"And when you're done with that, we need to schedule my meeting with the territorial governor in two weeks. Make sure my suits are cleaned and ready to go; I need to dress the part if I'm going to persuade him to make me a United States senator one day."

And just like that, Boyd had put Jed out of his mind. For him, it was always about the bigger picture; it was the one thing Jed never saw or understood. Most people would have a difficult time detaching themselves from a loved one's death—not Boyd. His real passion was the success of his businesses and his own ambitions.

EPILOGUE

ROCKLAND, IDAHO TERRITORY

SEPTEMBER 21, 1888

Abigail pulled the reins hard until her horse came to a full stop. She looked at Grant's farmhouse in the distance but hesitated before going down the drive. She had been rehearsing in her head how she'd tell George and Margaret about what had happened to their father. Of course, she hadn't seen his demise but had no doubt he didn't survive the diversion he'd orchestrated to save her life.

Having met them briefly before, she found George and Margaret polite, courteous and mature, but began to ponder how they'd handle such emotional news. Like her and even August, they were now members of a unique group of children that were parentless. The one thing they had that she didn't was each other; it was something she was envious of.

She heard the front door slam in the distance and saw a figure walk out. It appeared to be George. No doubt he was headed to the fields or barn to work.

Knowing that there wasn't a perfect way to tell them, she prayed his share of the bounty would ease their pain. She nudged her horse and turned it down the driveway.

George heard the galloping horse and stopped. He turned and walked back to the front of his house to await the rider. Upon seeing it was Abigail, an uneasy feeling swept over him. "Margaret, best come out here!" he hollered.

Margaret quickly appeared at the open doorway. She glanced at George then turned her head towards the drive when she heard the horse approaching. "Who is it?"

"It's Abigail," George replied.

Like George, Margaret felt a sense of doom wash over her.

Abigail slowed her horse to a trot and approached the siblings. When she came to a stop just feet from them, she nodded and removed her hat. "George, Margaret, good day."

"Where's Pa?" Margaret asked promptly.

Abigail didn't reply. She dismounted, opened her saddlebag, and removed a leather pouch.

"Where's Pa?" Margaret repeated.

With not only Grant's but August's share of the bounty in her possession, Abigail walked over to George and held it out. "This is for you and Margaret."

"What is it?" George asked, taking it.

"It's your father's share of the take from the bounty," Abigail answered.

"Where is he?" Margaret asked, marching towards Abigail.

"He's gone," Abigail replied, the look on her face telegraphing something had gone wrong.

"He's dead?" Margaret asked.

Abigail nodded.

Margaret began to cry.

George opened the bag, looked inside, and saw coins and a stack of bills. He looked at Abigail and asked, "What happened?"

"He saved my life."

"What does that mean?" Margaret wailed.

"He created a diversion so that I could escape and bring his share back to you," Abigail replied.

"I don't care about his share. I want my pa back," Margaret cried.

"He saved my life, and for that I'm eternally grateful, and I should tell you that he did this for you," Abigail said, feeling it wasn't necessary to go into detail.

"So he died an honorable death," George said, sounding proud.

"Yes, he did," Abigail confirmed.

"Honorable? There's nothing honorable about death," Margaret shrilled.

"My dear sister, Pa was dying anyway. He went and did this for us so that we may keep the farm and, by the looks of it, even expand it…"

"There's seven thousand dollars there," Abigail said, deliberately giving up some of her share so that they would have enough to survive.

"Thank you for bringing this back," George said.

"I can't believe he's gone," Margaret said.

"Me too," George said.

Abigail felt awkward; all she wanted to do now was leave. "I should go and let you two grieve."

"Why don't you stay tonight? You must be tired, and I bet you could use a hot meal and a warm bed," George offered. He was sad but resigned to the fact his father had died in such a way he was proud of. Like he'd promised, Grant had ensured they'd keep the farm and wouldn't be without. Now it was up to George to maintain it. Grant had passed the torch, and now George was the patriarch of the Toomey family, and he'd make sure to keep the family strong.

"Yes, please stay. Pa would want that," Margaret offered, putting aside her initial shock.

"Thank you for the offer, but I have somewhere to be," Abigail said, putting her hat back on.

"Are you sure?"

"Quite sure," she said, walking back to her horse.

"Where is his body?" Margaret asked.

"I don't know, but your pa would probably go by the old warriors' code of leaving him where he fell," Abigail said.

George nodded and said, "He would."

"We can't even bury him?" Margaret said, finding it hard to not even have a grave.

"Margaret, we can bury his stuff, will that suffice?" George asked.

Margaret gave George a slight nod. She faced Abigail and asked, "Are you sure you won't stay tonight?"

"Quite sure," Abigail said.

"How about taking some provisions with you?" George offered.

Abigail mounted her horse, settled into the saddle, and replied, "I'm fine. Please, you two have much to talk about and a farm to save."

George smiled. He looked around and said, "You're right."

"You take care," Abigail said, tipping her hat.

"Abby...I hope you don't mind me calling you that," George said.

"I only let family call me that, but for you I'll make an exception," she said, smiling.

"In my book, you are family. If my pa trusted you enough to take his last ride with you, that makes you family," George said. "And, Abby, you have a home here, a place to always come, a sanctuary of sorts; please know that."

Abigail's smile stretched further across her face. Those words meant a lot to her, more than she could ever say. "Thank you."

"Be safe, wherever you're riding," George said.

"I will," Abigail replied.

"By the way, where are you going?" Margaret asked.

"I've got to go help someone back in Billings," Abigail said, referring to the abused little girl, Madeleine, she'd come across recently.

"I hope it goes well for you," George said.

Abigail thought for a second then confidently said, "I think it will." She turned her horse around and rode off without saying another word.

George and Margaret watched her until she disappeared. They looked at each other then the sack full of coin and cash.

"I'll take this inside and put it in the secretary," George said, racing inside.

Margaret took a deep breath then exhaled with a sigh. Feelings of sadness, gratitude and hope all hit her simultaneously. She was sad she'd never see her father again, yet profoundly grateful for what he'd done for her and George, leaving her with a strong feeling of hope. He hadn't been the perfect father, but he did what parents were supposed to do, leave their children with a future.

WEST OF BILLINGS, MONTANA TERRITORY

SEPTEMBER 27, 1888

Loud banging at the front door woke the family.

Madeleine woke and looked over the edge of the loft, down into the living space of their cabin.

"Who the hell is banging on my door at this time of night?" the father hollered.

Fearful, Madeleine hid under a blanket, leaving only enough space to peek out.

More banging.

"Stop your damn banging!" the father roared as he got to the front door, unlocked it, and threw it open. He held up a lantern just in time to see the muzzle of a pistol come from the darkness. It rested on his forehead. The click of the hammer cocking back followed.

"Who are you? What do you want?"

Abigail stepped from the shadows and replied, "My name is Abby Sure Shot Bartlett, and I've come to take Madeleine."

Hearing her name, Madeleine popped her head up

out from underneath the blanket and looked closer at the person holding the pistol to her father's head. "Abigail?"

"Madeleine, you're coming with me," Abigail said.

Not hesitating, Madeleine grabbed her only beloved possession, a rag doll, and raced down the ladder and towards the front door.

Sophie exited the bedroom door and grabbed Madeleine by the arm. "You're not taking my baby girl."

"Let go of her. She's coming with me," Abigail said.

"No," Sophie screamed.

"Let go of me," Madeleine cried.

"You're not leaving to go with that stranger," Sophie said.

Madeleine lowered her head and bit Sophie's hand.

"Ouch!" Sophie cried out.

Breaking free from her mother's clutches, Madeleine ran past the stepfather to Abigail.

"Go outside," Abigail ordered.

Obedient, Madeleine did as she was told, leaving Abigail alone with her stepfather and mother.

"What kind of man gets pleasure out of beating children?" Abigail asked.

"She's an insolent, little—"

Not really wanting to hear him answer, Abigail smacked him in the mouth with the butt of her pistol. "Just shut up. Now, if I ever see you again, I'll put a nice hole right there," she said, tapping the muzzle against his forehead. "Do you understand?"

He nodded.

"And that goes for you, too," Abigail said to Sophie.

Sophie mumbled something unintelligible then began to sob.

Abigail stepped back and disappeared in the shadows from which she came. She ran to her horse and found Madeleine standing there. "Come, sweetheart," she said, picking her up and placing her in the saddle. She quickly mounted, keeping Madeleine in front of her, wrapped one arm around her small body, and rode off.

Once they were a safe distance away, Madeleine said, "You came back, you came back to help me."

"You're all I've thought about since the day I saw you. I couldn't rest until I got you out of that house."

"Where are we going?" Madeleine asked.

Abigail pondered the question; she hadn't put much thought into it before. "I don't know, but I can assure you that it'll be somewhere safe."

THE END

ABOUT THE AUTHOR

G. Michael Hopf is the best-selling author of THE NEW WORLD series and other apocalyptic novels. He spent two decades living a life of adventure before he settled down and became a novelist full time. He is a combat veteran of the Marine Corps and a former executive protection agent.

He lives with his family in San Diego, CA
Please feel free to contact him at geoff@gmichaelhopf.com with any questions or comments.
www.gmichaelhopf.com
www.facebook.com/gmichaelhopf

Books by G. MICHAEL HOPF

THE NEW WORLD SERIES

THE END
THE LONG ROAD
SANCTUARY
THE LINE OF DEPARTURE
BLOOD, SWEAT & TEARS
THE RAZOR'S EDGE
THOSE WHO REMAIN

NEW WORLD SERIES SPIN OFFS

NEMESIS: INCEPTION
EXIT

THE WANDERER SERIES

VENGEANCE ROAD
BLOOD GOLD
TORN ALLEGIANCE

ADDITIONAL BOOKS
HOPE (CO-AUTHORED W/ A. AMERICAN)
DAY OF RECKONING
MOTHER (EXTINCTION CYCLE SERIES)
DETACHMENT (PERSEID COLLAPSE SERIES)
DRIVER 8: A POST-APOCALYPTIC NOVEL

89804332R00149

Made in the USA
Middletown, DE
18 September 2018